ESTATE

OF

DESPAIRS

PERSEPHONE PRINGLE COZY MYSTERIES: SIX

PATTI LARSEN

Thanks, Kirstin!

ISBN: 978-1-989925-81-2

CHAPTER ONE

"Trick or treat!" The adorable space alien held out his green bucket, the DIY mask with the giant eyes lopsided on his little face, full body suit rolled up at the wrists and ankles, clearly meant for someone bigger. Not that it mattered a little bit, mind you. I offered up my best cackle, the orange light bulb I'd installed over the entry reflecting on the excessive and glamorous makeup I'd used to enhance the elegant eyeliner and massive lashes (don't forget a bucketload of sparkles and deep pink lips). I fluttered said lashes while dumping a handful of candy into his already half-full bucket. "Thank you!" He spun and ran back down the walk to the street, his mother waving at me as I waved back, barely closing the door to refill my stash when the doorbell rang again.

I adjusted my giant, black witch's hat in the hall mirror before opening the door with an enthusiastic, "Happy Halloween!" for my newest spooks. Two picture-perfect princesses in their fluffy gowns and sparkling tiaras chimed in tandem.

"Trick or treat!" More treats changed hands while their parents waited at the gate, friendly waves returned when the twins pranced their way to carry on their treasure hunt.

Belladonna chirped from behind the closed kitchen door, and I knew I'd suffer horribly for locking her away for the evening. Thing was, despite the cutesy unicorn costume I'd bought her, she not only refused to wear it, she hated her harness. Since she loved to escape and did so at the least convenient times, it was either trap her in the house or spend the night looking for her instead of handing out treats.

"It's almost 8PM," I called out to her, tugging unceremoniously on my pink and black striped tights before smoothing the short, excessive crinoline skirt I'd added over them under the black velvet corset and short velvet cape. My time in the gym and strict no-carb eating had finally pushed me into the realm of feeling kind of hot and almost to my goal so I took a vain moment to admire myself—and my blonde bob wig—in the mirror with a faint giggle I couldn't suppress.

Honestly, I needed to grow up. But who wanted to when life was this fun?

Two more rings and the night was over, Wallace's town curfew sending the kids home to gorge on chocolate and pass out in a sugar coma while their parents secreted the rest away (or ate them themselves—hey, guilty once upon a time). I sadly turned out the light, shedding my hat as I opened the door to the house, Belladonna yowling her frustration at me in one long and clearly planned out yodel of her discontent.

"Yes, please," I said, striding past her in my witchy button-up boots. "Sing me the song of your angst. I'm all ears."

She followed me into the kitchen, hopping up on the counter, continuing to mutter and crank until I opened her a can of tuna.

"Funny how little it takes," I said, slipping out of one of the mesh gloves I wore to stroke her fur, "and all's forgiven."

She purred her happiness, though I was positive this was only a momentary truce. She'd find a way to make sure I understood the error of my ways and how terrible a human I was.

I leaned on the counter, staring at the clock, a little sad Halloween was, for all intents and purposes, over for me. My efforts to recruit anyone to come with me to the dance party going on at the local hall were met with a chorus of denials from all corners, including, to my surprise, my mother and her husband, Ralph.

Only because they had plans. "We're off to Portland for the zombie walk," Mom told me, giggling as she backhanded Ralph in the arm, her favorite gesture of endearment. "We learned that zombie dance, you know the one I mean?" Of course, she had, the popular pop song about Halloween all the rage no matter how old it was. "Did you want to come, honey?"

I'd turned her down, deciding maybe getting dressed up and going out was past its expiry date for me and I'd be much happier spending a quiet night with Belladonna.

Right. Because it was only my favorite thing in the whole world to dress up, go out and dance at every opportunity. Add in the chance to be whoever I wanted for a night?

"Oh well, sweet girl," I said as Belladonna finished her tuna, still purring. "Silly to stand here dressed like this and feel sorry for myself." I'd considered buying a ticket and going to the dance solo, except nothing was sadder than the one lone desperate divorcee on the dancefloor surrounded by couples.

Not a good reason to have a boyfriend or anything, but there were times in the last year I contemplated dating just so I'd have someone to go to events with.

My phone buzzed, a text coming in. I checked it immediately, anything to distract me from the self-pity I seemed to have fallen into. *Hey, Mom.* Weird for Calliope to just send a short greeting like that. Hard not to feel hope in the shadow of my poor me moment since the girls were hosting a party themselves at Vesterville House. Only the perfect venue for such a party. While I wasn't a fan of the towering pile of stone and icy coldness that was Thalia Vesterville's ancestral home, at least it was good for something one night a year.

Bring on the creep factor. Vesterville House had it in spades.

Of course, they'd invited me, sweet of them do to so, right? I'd turned them down, though, because sadder than a lone chick at a couple's event? A cougar at a twentysomething party. Yeah, as much as it would have been a blast, (and it would) I couldn't bring myself to hang out with kids half my age (and less), whether my daughter and her girlfriend asked me to come or not.

I normally didn't care what people thought of me but, come on. Yikes. I'd either come across as a desperate old lady looking for arm candy or a chaperone.

Not in this lifetime, Persephone Pringle.

Hi, sweetie, I sent. *Need something for the party?* So desperate, really. But no one could judge me for just picking up a few things for them and dropping them off and staying for one drink and maybe dancing a little… right?

Pathetic.

You know how you said if I thought it was time Lia needed help? Okay, yikes. That I wasn't expecting. Thalia had been showing classic signs of depression for over two months now, and though I'd offered in the past to help (not directly, if she wanted to talk to someone else, even), Calliope and her need for privacy after a lifetime of being watched by her FBI agent father and therapy Mom'd by yours truly, put her foot down and pretty much cut both of us out of her decision-making process. Which was totally fair, except, of course, that meant endless worry for Thalia and her state of mental health.

Things had seemed to improve since they'd opted for a long, cross-country train ride in September before renting a car and driving back. Thalia even seemed almost back to herself, and I'd thought this party meant she was continuing to feel better. I should have realized, though, since I saw her so rarely these days, that her issues wouldn't be so readily resolved.

I'd backed off, but was it the right choice? Apparently not. No guilt about it or anything.

What do you need, Callie? I left that question hanging, held my breath, wished she'd hurry and reply as my anxiety decided to take control and set me pacing across the kitchen and back, my boots clicking on the tile floor.

Can you come? The only way Calliope would ask was if something had happened, something that scared her or pushed her through her need to live her own life into panic.

She only had to ask. *On my way.*

CHAPTER TWO

I was half expecting the influx of guests to have begun, forgetting that anyone under the age of thirty didn't call 8ish PM party time. When did I get old again? While fifty (almost one) honestly felt like twenty-five, certain things just didn't function the same. Like bedtime.

Yup. Old. Get over it.

The fact the youngsters (snort) disagreed with my internal clock meant hopefully I'd arrived in time to be of assistance, at least. My choice to leave Belladonna home still had me doubting, knowing how much Thalia loved her and took comfort from her presence. But with all those potential people doing the in-and-out thing, I knew the cat would take full advantage of the opportunity to skedaddle when the whim took her. Thalia's staff had already proven unable to restrain the floof from having her own way and choosing one of the myriad exits from the giant mansion into the gardens beyond. Having to worry about Belladonna would take away from my real reason for being here. I wanted (and needed, quite frankly) to focus on the girls, not chasing that silly fluff creature across Vesterville Estate in the dark while swearing at her and wishing I'd left her home.

Sorry, Bella.

I parked off to the side, knowing the circular drive would be packed with cars over the next few hours, hoping to keep my SUV in the clear so I could make a getaway once things wound up. If they wound up. I'd grabbed my hat if only to disguise the reason I was really there because in balance between exposing Thalia and struggling with looking like a cougar? You better believe I chose my second daughter.

It wasn't lost on me as I strode up the steps to the large double doors the party might be over before it even got started.

Lloyd Mitchem answered immediately to the booming chime of the bell, the last strains of it echoing back to me through the doorway as he bowed his head in welcome. While he may have been Vesterville's butler, he was also retired CIA, so I had no doubt he was capable of not just serving the girls but assuring they were safe and sound. Still, the sadness on his face when he ushered me inside wasn't all that secret agent man. If anything, his emotional attachment to Thalia and Calliope seemed stronger than his old training.

"This way, Ms. Pringle," he said, hurrying me along toward the stairs. "I'm afraid they've been fighting for the last hour and things aren't improving whatsoever." Fighting? My girls? "Thank you so much for coming so quickly. I know Miss Calliope will be happy to see you."

"What are they fighting about?" I'd never once, not since they were little girls together, seen the pair of them argue over anything. Calliope's boundless, sunny energy always seemed to counterbalance Thalia's introverted quiet shyness to the point they just fit together perfectly. Which was why I was happy they'd finally come out as a couple. The idea they were fighting had my pulse racing, worry I'd stepped off a terrible mistake we'd all live to regret.

"Miss Thalia has become increasingly volatile in the last two weeks," Lloyd said, keeping his voice down, setting a pace that would have pushed the cardio of a man thirty years his junior. I know I was panting a little despite my gym time, blamed it on the high-heeled boots, as he went on. "Since they returned from their trip, she has fallen deeper into her sorrow. Only it's turned now into irritability and aggression." He stopped suddenly at the top of the stairs to the third floor, facing me. "I don't mean to speak ill of my mistress, but I'm very worried about her, Persephone." That was the first time he'd ever used my first name. "I realize Miss Calliope would prefer you to stay out of it, but I think the time for that has come to an end. Something must be done, or I fear we will lose Miss Thalia to the curse of the Vesterville's, a real thing or only in her mind or not."

Nice of someone to finally be honest with me. Okay, so maybe Calliope had opened up somewhat a couple of months ago, but since then she'd clammed up again, leaving me even more worried since I now knew for certain she was in trouble and any attempt to visit was policed by my own daughter. Not that Calliope wanted Thalia to suffer, I was certain, but her need for personal space was taking things too far. Thankfully I could finally take action and I couldn't freaking wait. "I'll do everything I can, Lloyd," I said. "They're in their room?" I knew where to go from here.

He nodded, glancing that way, misery on his

face. "If anyone can help her." He turned back, squeezed my hand with his white-gloved one. "Shall I turn the guests away as they arrive?"

I didn't want to make that choice for the girls, not without assessing the situation personally. "I'll let you know," I said. "Let them in for now but be aware we might have to send them away if things go badly."

He immediately bowed again before turning and hurrying down the stairs, leaving me to catch my breath—mentally and physically—before I strode the length of the arching, dark-paneled corridor lined with judging and dubiously pretentious Vesterville portraits to the main suite doors.

One thing about Lloyd, he wasn't a kidder, straight-shooting as they came. As if I required proof of his honesty, when I neared the entry I could hear them, if faintly, even through the heavy double portal to the main suite of the third floor. Oh, and not just a wee tad of noise, oh no. It was clearly and audibly a full-blown fight unfolding behind those doors. In fact, they were so dedicated to their yelling match, I was able to sweep through and into the front sitting room and past the doorway to the bedroom without either of them noticing I'd arrived. Hopefully to save the day, if not Thalia from further pain and my daughter from her ridiculous need to take matters into her own hands and refuse help.

Yes, she got her stubbornness from me, so I could hardly blame her for her attitude. And yet, I wasn't the one facing off with the love of my life, red in the face, arms waving, while said girlfriend did the same.

I barely caught bits and pieces of the argument that had reached the point where it wailed at a decibel and pitch that hurt my ears and made it hard to understand. Clearly, they'd been at it a while, so hopefully they were at the peak of the wave and were ready to come down. Still, despite their loud, garbled and overlapping shrieking, there was sufficient wordage coming through for me to at least get the gist if not the full story behind the fight. "Stop mothering me!" from Thalia and "You're impossible!" from Calliope seemed to be at the core of the whole thing. It was obvious they'd come to some kind of emotional cliff and were about to push one another over.

It turned out, even with my desire to do so, there was no need to intervene, at least not with my shout for attention. Because the moment I stopped and drew a breath to do just that, Thalia crumpled, collapsing into a chair next to the bed, while my daughter hurried forward, her round cheeks red from anger, worry replacing it so fast I knew it wasn't real temper that had Calliope worked up, but fear.

Thalia pushed her away, pale cheeks that translucent whiteness I'd noticed lately, cheeks hollow and big, blue eyes sunken. She'd dressed for the party in an old WWII uniform, one I knew belonged to Abigail Spelling, an old friend of her great-grandfather and the inspiration for her Uncle Graves. Not to mention the source of a family murder, but that was beside the point. While it was lovely she'd chosen to honor Abigail by wearing her uniform—the infamous spy she'd been would have been delighted, I was sure—it was far too close for comfort where the curse and the history of the Vestervilles were concerned. While it could have been a tribute, why did I get the feeling Thalia instead stepped into the dress of the past because of her terror the family's curse was coming for her?

CHAPTER THREE

I joined them, sitting beside Thalia who looked up and blinked at me, expression rather dazed, taking a moment to recognize me, even. I held her hand while she finally came back all the way and hugged me with a low cry that sounded far too hurt for my liking.

Calliope's hazel eyes had brimmed with tears, my pirate captain daughter's giant feathered hat discarded and waiting on the bed, the thick black leather belt and matching sea boots adorable, as was the tight black vest and pants and her puffy white shirt. I would have appreciated her dangling eyepatch and the sword at her side more if it weren't for the present state of affairs.

"Make her leave just me alone." Thalia's whimpering request had me asking Calliope silent questions my daughter just shrugged in response to. Oh, she knew exactly what was on my mind, had been reading my silent questions her whole young life, so this nonverbal communication was nothing new. If Thalia noticed, she didn't show it, the Vesterville heiress leaning away from me, twisting her body sideways so she didn't have to look at Calliope. "She won't leave me alone. She's always on me about something." Thalia's temper returned with every word she spoke until she surged to her feet, my daughter standing to face off with her. Again, it would have been comical, a pirate and a WWII soldier/spy, if it wasn't so freakishly surreal. "Go to the doctor." Her tone shifted to mocking. "You're not all right. There's something wrong with you. Why won't you listen to me? There's no such thing as a curse." Thalia tossed her hands, spinning away from Calliope and staring at me with a wild and feral expression on her face, two bright pink points of heat on the sharp protrusions of her cheekbones, sunken blue eyes flaring with anger. "For the very last time, I'm fine. I don't need to see anyone. *You* aren't listening to *me*." That hit the mark, my daughter twitching like she wanted to protest. "If you can't or won't believe me, why are you even here?" And it had gone that far, had it? Not good. "*You* think there's something wrong with *me*? At least I'm not nagging *you*." Yikes, they sounded like an old married couple. "All I want is for you to listen to me, to believe me, to trust me, but you *don't*." Thalia's rant had come to a crest at last. "So, if you won't, why don't you just leave me alone!" She stormed off and I let her, catching Calliope when she tried to go after her, tugging her down next to me on the sofa and hugging her, rocking her, while my daughter cried.

"Mom, she's getting worse," she whispered, choking out the words before pulling away to reach for a tissue from the box on the end table. The bedroom's four-poster king-sized bed barely made a dent in the giant footprint of the space, two sofas, four chairs and a small writing desk trying to fill the rest of the space, a giant fireplace the only other object in the room that seemed to take up sufficient room to belong. "I should have listened to you. I'm sorry, I'm an idiot. Thalia's not okay and it's my fault."

I hugged her again, fought her resistance until she relaxed a little. "Tell me."

"I think..." Calliope sniffed, dabbed at her nose with the tissue. "Mom, I think she's taking drugs." Thalia?" She sat back when I let her, surprise loosening my grip. Those hazel eyes had enough fear in them I held my tongue and let her go on. "She acts, I don't know, like kind of stoned a lot." She shook her head, hiccupping softly through the tears that continued to fall. "I can't explain it. One second she's quiet and Thalia and the next, boom." She tossed her hands. "She loses it. Then when the tantrum is over, she goes back to quiet, only she's sleepy, as if she hasn't slept in weeks. Mom, she's had a checkup, but that was two months ago. The doctor said she was fine. So, I can't think of what else it might be."

I could. Psychotic breaks were uncommon with depression, but not unheard of. For her to have developed psychotic depression and I hadn't acted…? More guilt layered on the regret and despair I'd failed her. If it was that diagnosis, Thalia needed hospitalization before she deteriorated further.

"We should cancel the party," I said. "Thalia needs to go to the hospital right now."

"I'm not going anywhere." She'd returned, apparently, facing off with both of us. Instead of freaking out on me, however, Thalia took a deep breath and spread her hands at her sides. "I know you think I'm having a breakdown," she said to both of us. "But did you ever think maybe I'm finally letting out the emotions that I never had the chance to? When was the last time you saw me angry?" I didn't answer, Calliope shaking her head in visible misery. "Or really excited about something?" Again, there was nothing I could say and nothing my daughter would. Thalia sagged, looking like a little girl wearing her mother's clothes for a moment, and I almost rose and went to her then and there. But when she straightened, her narrow shoulders going back, chin rising, she filled out the decorated uniform jacket far better than I expected. "For the last time, Callie," she said, "I'm not taking anything. No drugs, prescription or otherwise. Okay?"

Honestly, I was far more reassured than Calliope. First of all, there was no way this was my first conclusion jump into abysmal. She wouldn't have been able to resurface from psychotic depression like this. That didn't mean she wasn't in the midst of a mental health crisis, however, no matter what she said to the contrary. But at least it wasn't imminently important to admit and sedate her so she didn't hurt herself or someone else.

"Mom's right," Calliope said, tentative now as if expecting to be attacked. "We should just cancel, Lia."

"This party was your idea." There was her temper again, Thalia's body shaking with it. "You wanted me to be more social, to see people. You pushed me." She struck both thighs with her fists, jaw jumping, cords in her neck standing out. Thalia tilted her head to one side, closing her eyes, lips a thin line before she pulled herself together enough to go on. "We're having this party so everyone you seem to think matters knows I'm not a freak."

"Lia." Calliope stood, hand stretched out to her girlfriend, distress in her voice, enough pain for both of them. "I never said that."

"You don't have to." Again with the head tilt, a soft and subtle shake following before Thalia opened her eyes. "It doesn't matter. We're having this party." She turned and left, striding from the room, while I tried to categorize everything I'd seen and slot each detail into a space that made sense.

Except nothing I'd witnessed did.

Calliope turned to me, desperate hope in her face. "Tell me you can help her." She sobbed once, body shaking with it, silent weeping firing up again before she drew a ragged and harsh breath. "Mom, I can't believe I was so selfish. You could have been helping her all along and I was so wrapped up in being my own person and doing things for myself I think I ruined this." She hugged herself tight. "I think I lost the only person I'll ever love."

No need for such panic just yet. My fears

had diminished enough I could get a grip on hysteria, at least, even if my daughter couldn't. Whatever was going on with Thalia, as long as she was willing, we could find a way to guide her through it.

"Callie," I said, standing and hugging her again, rocking her a little, "you've been here for her. That's what matters. We'll deal with the rest of it as it happens. Okay?" She sniffled, nodded. "She's determined to have the party, so let's do that. No more antagonizing her, all right? And when this is over and we can sit down and talk, we will. It's going to be okay, sweetie."

"Can you please stay?" Silly daughter child. Calliope asked me that like she thought I was going somewhere.

CHAPTER FOUR

I left her to clean herself up, in pursuit of Thalia. While her startling return to sort of normal after the temper tantrum I'd witnessed eliminated the fear of a total breakdown, something was definitely wrong and until I had a chance to talk to her privately, to ask her details she might only disclose to me (or not, we'd see), I wouldn't know if I should be calling an ambulance or pouring myself a gin and cranberry to get through tonight.

Hopefully, the latter because I was so ready for a drink.

There was no sign of Thalia when I reached the foyer, though a number of guests had arrived, Lloyd and two of the staff guiding them through the foyer and into the ballroom. I bypassed the trio of sexy nurses and their doctor boyfriends, waiting for them to enter the large double doors before poking my nose in.

And almost ran right into a young woman in a black and white French maid costume, her green-dyed bob the same color as her contact lenses, the intensity of the color startling to say the least. Not to mention the lip, nose and eyebrow piercings and the lacework of delicate tattoos that circled her neck and ran down her chest under the suggestively, and purposeful, aggressive cleavage of her uniform.

"Looking for someone?" She couldn't have been more than twenty, though the black makeup and lipstick made it hard to be sure.

"Thalia," I smiled back. "I'm Persephone Pringle, Calliope's mother."

Her eyes widened, smile showing the small gap between her front teeth. "You're Callie's mom, huh?" She took a step back, looked me up and down, whistled and winked. "Pretty hot for fifty, Ms. P. Nice tats."

And who might she be? I grinned back. "I love your hair," I said.

"Thanks." She shrugged at me, the large, round silver tray in her hands now under one arm, fishnets ending in platform heels that would have made me fall just looking at them. "And you have no idea who I am." That seemed to amuse her to no end.

"I'm sorry," I said. "But you're going to tell me, right?"

"Maybe," she said with a sly smile. Then snorted a little laugh. "Just kidding. I'm Brin Anderson. Melanie's daughter."

Oh.

Oh, okay then.

I must have looked like she slapped me because she hooted at my shock, catching the attention of a couple of beauty queens with crowns and sashes who strode by in floor-length gowns and perfect updos. Brin ignored them, not seeming to care they observed her reaction with disdain. I liked her already.

"Nice to meet you," she said. "Trent says great things about you." Did he now? Though my ex-husband and I weren't exactly friends, there'd been no animosity outside his poking his nose into Callie's business to generate anything to the contrary, so I suppose I shouldn't have been surprised. But I was, frankly, that he'd brought me up at all to his new girlfriend and her daughter.

"I'm happy to finally meet you," I said. Had a thought. "Your mother's catering?"

Brin nodded, held out the tray. "I'm serving," she said, leaning in with a cynical twist to her lips. "Heaven forbid I fit in here enough to get an invite." She eye-rolled then laughed like she couldn't care less. And I believed it.

"I don't exactly fit in either," I said.

"Well, stay away from the boys, Ms. P.," she said with enough suggestiveness I snorted. "Wouldn't want to catch anything." She bopped off, her platform shoes making her legs look like stilts, as she carried on out of the ballroom and into the foyer.

Calliope had mentioned Brin to me once. Only once. I'd gotten the impression there might be tension there. Trouble was, for the life of me? I couldn't understand why. Brin seemed down to earth and casually confident in herself, just like Calliope.

Huh. Maybe that was the problem. Too much alike?

Not my problem *du jour*. One issue at a time, thank you.

I spotted Thalia at the far end of the ballroom, but she wasn't alone. And, to my surprise, had a drink in her hand, though she was old enough, of course, she was. Twenty-two was hardly underage. Still, Thalia wasn't normally a drinker, and this was the second time I'd seen her with wine in her hand. Then again, I hadn't seen much of her, had I, in the last two months? She and Calliope had been keeping to themselves.

That was over, no matter if my kid changed her mind or not. They were not getting rid of me until Thalia was sorted.

Calliope stopped next to me, a glass of beer in one hand, worry all over her face. My daughter had never been good at hiding how she felt, and tonight was no exception. Considering the focus of her attention, I'd have been worried if she could pretend. "Did you want me to ask her to come over?"

"No," I said. "Why don't you do your thing. I'm just going to watch her for a little while. Okay?" She nodded, looking dubious enough, but obeyed me, crossing to Thalia and joining her. I noticed she tried to take her girlfriend's hand, only to be rejected. The blush that rose on Calliope's cheeks before she turned away hurt me so much, I wished I had convinced Thalia to shut down the party after all.

I spent the next hour or so shadowing her, staying to the periphery, and was honestly surprised by what I saw. Thalia, for the first time in her short existence, was the life of the party. She chatted, she laughed, she made others laugh. And while she continually sipped her wine, there was no massive intake of alcohol, no excessive imbibing I witnessed, and no real show of drunken behavior or lack of control aside from her oddly uncharacteristic extroversion.

Whatever was up, maybe she was right. Could she simply be doing what she said, embracing how she felt, finally letting her true self out? I often wondered if the reserved and quiet little girl she'd been, the sadly lonely and retreating young woman might not have a far different personality if she'd only been allowed to flourish instead of being neglected by those who were supposed to love and raise her. Losing her parents so young hadn't helped and though Trent and I stepped in as best we could, the loss and the subsequent issues with her horrible family had ended in a reclusive woman I adored but wished I could have done more for.

Here was the Thalia I'd always imagined she could be, showing up and surprising me and, it seemed, everyone else, too. By the time 9:30 rolled around, I was starting to think maybe Lloyd and Calliope mistook Thalia's evolution for psychopathy.

I managed five minutes alone with her, Thalia beaming a smile at me, rather breathless after a short spin around the dancefloor as the space started to fill up.

"I love your costume choice," I said with my own smile. It made me think about a certain private email address I'd been granted access to almost a year ago, an address I'd never contacted. "Abigail would have loved it." So would her Uncle Gaines.

She hugged me with one arm, the other holding her wine glass at a distance. "I'm not taking drugs," she whispered in my ear. "I swear."

"I believe you," I whispered back. "She's just worried. You're changing and she doesn't know what to do."

Thalia leaned away, nodded, faint smile fading. "I know," she said. "Neither do I, sometimes. But this is who I am now." Thalia tossed her head. "It's been a long year, Seph. I've come through a lot." That anger was back, but it felt off to me, her eyes slightly unfocused and wait, what was that head tilt about? "If she can't deal with that, maybe we weren't meant for one another." She turned and left me to deal with that while I sighed over the fact I might be comforting my daughter very shortly when her girlfriend broke up with her.

That was going to be fun.

All thoughts of breakups and impending relationship crash and burns ground to an immediate halt the moment I turned to head back to the foyer.

Stopped dead in my tracks.

And ground my teeth at the sight of a handsome young man in a suit—he hadn't even bothered to dress up, naturally—with a posse of sycophants rushing to his side as he entered the ballroom like he owned Vesterville House.

Raised an uncomfortable question I wasn't ready to answer. If Thalia wasn't doing drugs, why was notorious and, as yet, uncharged drug dealer Rider Huntington at her party?

CHAPTER FIVE

Calliope seemed to be wondering the same thing, my kid heading directly for the grinning trust fund jerkface, and while I understood her expression to the core of my soul—all anger and all determined heck no—I wasn't so sure she of the almost 5'2" was the best choice to tackle an alleged drug princepin and possible murderer on her own, dressed as a pirate captain or not.

The fact she looked rather ridiculous stomping her *argh matey* way toward him, that gigantic feather bobbing from her black hat, did nothing to slow her steps, nor mine as I hoofed it as fast as I could to catch her before she did something Cherise would be forced to arrest her for.

Thalia appeared at my side as I stopped next

to Calliope, one hand on her arm, while my daughter's shaking increased, though out of anger, not fear, that much was absolutely certain.

"You're not welcome here," she snarled at Rider who gave her a slow up and down look that spoke all kinds of volumes of judgment and derision, smirk pulling his handsome face into a rather ugly expression that did nothing for his good looks and painted him as exactly the arrogant and pompously entitled brat he was.

"You don't get to tell Rider what to do." The young woman on his arm, dressed in a slinky black number with high heels and so many glittering bits and pieces from her necklace to the drops in her curled black hair she cast rainbows from the lights.

"Perhaps not," Thalia said, cool and composed. "But I do."

The young woman turned to the Vesterville heiress with a smug smile on her face. "Thalia," she said, dragging out her name. "Hello, darling. Thanks for the invite. You know we can only stop by for a minute, right?"

"Joslyn," Thalia said, just as chill and unwelcoming. "How lovely of you to invite yourself despite the fact you know you're not welcome."

The black-haired beauty (on the outside) simply tossed her head, while the tall, muscular man on Rider's left stepped in.

"Hey, Lia," he said, no posturing, just a shrug under his own dress jacket, the trio clearly above dressing up for Halloween. "We don't want trouble. Just figured it might be fun."

"It has been, Lawson," Callie snapped, "until you three walked through the door." She turned to Thalia, hands fisted at her sides. "I'll have Lloyd escort them out."

I had no doubt in my mind whatsoever if Calliope had kept her mouth shut the three of them would have been summarily dismissed from Vesterville House without another thought about it. But I saw my daughter's commanding attempt to take charge shift Thalia's attitude, watched her rebellion wake and the sullen response to her girlfriend's attempt to protect her turn Thalia from quiet command in her own right to rejection of whatever Calliope wanted in that moment.

With her head tilting to the left (what was that? It looked like a tic, almost triggered by her shift in mood), Thalia abruptly waved Calliope off, not even looking at her while my daughter gaped and turned redder than she had been. "You're welcome to stay," she said, offhand

and rather rude, completely out of character for the young woman I'd known most of her life. "But don't make trouble or I'll throw you all out myself."

Calliope spluttered before her scowl turned to hurt fury. Thalia turned away from her, walked off, leaving the trio of new guests to carry on. And don't think I missed the fact that Joslyn purposely bumped my daughter's shoulder with her own, laughing as she passed her.

I watched them cross the ballroom, struggling with a myriad of my own emotions and the need to do something. Not the least of my worries was Thalia's immensely odd behavior. But having someone like Rider Huntington in the house meant trouble.

Movement near the far wall where the table laid out with finger foods and fresh glasses stood caught my attention. Even more so the shock on Brin's face at the sight of the three. She stood frozen a long moment before she spun and hurried from the room, brushing past me as if not seeing me.

Making it very clear she had history with one or all three of them. Was that the source of Calliope's concern about her father's potential stepdaughter?

"Mom," my kid quickly closed the distance

between us, still trembling though from the last of the adrenaline I was sure, because her anger was gone, replaced by misery. "What's wrong with her?"

I shook my head, wishing now I'd urged her to cancel the party. "I don't know, Calliope," I said. "I understand her reasoning, that she's trying to embrace who she never got to be. But there's something even more off about her now than when she was fighting depression." At least in the darkness she'd been herself, to a point. I didn't recognize this young woman at all and that had me very worried.

Psychotic breaks could show in a myriad of ways and just because I hadn't seen this particular variance before didn't mean we weren't dealing with a total meltdown of Thalia's personality.

"I need to call Cherise." Calliope flinched, shook her head. "Thalia will never forgive me."

"Then I'll call," I said, hugging her around the shoulders with one arm. "She can hate me all she wants."

My daughter's gratitude barely made a dent in her anxiety but at least it was a start. She hurried off toward Thalia, though I was certain she was about to make herself even more miserable if she tried to talk reason to her girlfriend.

I quickly texted Cherise the details, as a heads up. Waited near the doors as more guests arrived, keeping to the side and out of the way until the sheriff's text came back.

Thanks for the warning, she sent. *I can't spare anyone right now. Freaking Halloween.* Right, she and her deputies would have their hands full, curfew or no curfew. *I've got complaints all over town about eggings and toilet paper carnage.* I could almost hear her snort in amusement at the childish pranks. *He causing trouble?*

Not yet, I sent back.

Keep an eye on him and me posted and I'll be there ASAP.

Fair enough.

Now, she'd said keep an eye on him, right? That implied *stay out of his way and don't make the situation worse until she could get here and deal with him herself.* That was an absolutely logical supposition, wasn't it? Which meant, naturally, I ignored the *mind your business, Seph* part and instead took a stroll to the back end of the ballroom where Rider helped himself to a flute of champagne.

He watched me approach, gaze lazy and cavalier, but when I came to a stop next to him his eyes widened, his normal smirk fading to a flash of anger that pleased me to no end.

"Couldn't help notice your bodyguards

aren't hanging around anymore," I said. "Unless you count those two." I gestured at Joslyn, his equally haughty date chatting with someone she deemed worthy, the two girls dressed as beauty queens, no less. His other companion, Lawson, stood to one side, observing me talking to his friend with an unhappy and unwelcoming expression but did nothing to interfere.

"Who needs bodyguards when you're innocent of wrongdoing?" Rider's smooth comeback ended in his gaze flickering away at the end, clear indication he was angry, and lying. Sometimes having the kind of training I did meant I learned more from his body language than his speech.

"If you say so," I said, letting him hear the taunt in my tone. "I just figured your bosses didn't find you all that important to their business anymore."

Rider snarled into his glass, then shrugged. "I've parted ways with my previous… partners," he said. Met my gaze with his own full of bitter rage. "Thanks to you and that sheriff of yours." Nice to be helpful, wasn't it? I almost grinned despite knowing how dangerous that would be. Despite his rich boy entitlement, I was well aware Rider was capable of truly horrible crimes, so teasing him really was a terrible idea. Except I couldn't bring myself to take this manchild seriously.

"You're welcome," I said because I couldn't help myself.

"I owe you one, Persephone Pringle," he said, the threat in his voice matching the fury in his eyes.

"Rider." I hadn't noticed until then Lawson's approach, his right-hand man with a firm grasp on the furious drug dealer's arm. "We don't want trouble, remember?" Lawson met my eyes with his brown ones under heavy brows raised under the wave of his artfully arranged dark hair, nodding. "Ms. Pringle."

The fact Lawson knew who I was didn't comfort me. "We haven't met," I said, sticking out my hand with a reflexive smile to which he instantly responded, shaking mine.

"Lawson Derrick," he said. "I went to school with Callie."

"Looks like you're keeping different company these days," I said. "You might want to reconsider your choices." I beamed a smile at Rider. "Have a nice evening. At least, until Cherise King gets here." So fun, really, too much fun. "The sheriff will be along shortly."

"I'm a welcome guest on private property," Rider said, his pomposity returning. "And you two can think all you like you interfered with my business." That came out in a fresh snarl. "But there are new opportunities around every corner, aren't there?" He fished his phone out of his pocket as it hummed, checked the screen. You know what was weird? We had the exact same one, case and all, dead black and built to withstand a tank driving over it. Go figure. He, meanwhile, grinned at me, tight and feral. "Now, if you'll excuse me, I have a party to enjoy and you're not welcome."

I let him walk away, strut, actually, Lawson waving a little behind his back, making me wonder what the obviously nice young man was doing with someone like Rider and, more so, what the young Huntington meant about new opportunities.

Did I think about Thalia and her newfound self? You better believe it. But, for the time being, there wasn't anything I could do about it. Except keep my eyes on Rider, right?

Yes, Cherise.

Eyes it was. Unless he did something to threaten my girls. Then she'd better turn her own away because she wasn't going to watch what happened next.

CHAPTER SIX

I circled the table to get out of the way, looking for a good vantage point to watch the whole party without being obvious about it. That meant I saw Melanie Anderson enter the ballroom with Brin at her side, watched the pair of them hiss angrily at one another before Brin firmly dragged her mother away.

I'd uncovered not so long ago that Trent's girlfriend was on anti-anxiety meds, namely Zexan. I considered going after them and asking what was up when my phone buzzed.

Layla and her friends are on their way to Vesterville House, Cherise sent. *I told her to steer clear, but she refused to answer my texts*. Like my own kid (kids, as of now), Layla had been pushing her mother's boundaries lately. Only a year behind Calliope and Thalia, now officially twenty-one and more than happy to have a few beers unlike her older counterparts, she'd clearly been taking lessons from my daughter at least, her plan to take the winter semester off and go traveling already arranged and her flight paid for with her earnings from her job at The Blueberry Grill. It didn't surprise me she was blocking her mother's demanding texts.

I'll watch for her, I sent. *But right now, honestly, Rider and his two friends are just socializing.* I didn't mention his new opportunities comment because she had a job to do and the last thing she needed was to be worrying about Layla. *I doubt they'd try anything at a party like this.*

They might be selling, Cherise sent back.

Not as far as I can tell, I sent, *but if I see anything change hands, they're out of here. Okay?*

Thanks, Seph, she replied. *I'll try to hurry.*

Yeah, Layla was going to love Cherise showing up about as much as Calliope would if the situations were flipped. Thing was, we needed to let them live their own lives, yes, but allowing them to walk head-first into danger just wasn't on the dance card.

They could lump it.

I spent the next hour observing like the dreaded high school chaperone I felt like, turning down an offer of a gin and cranberry from Lloyd when he joined me a moment.

"I'm happy to step in at any time," he said. "Just give me the word, Ms. Pringle."

He might have been in his sixties, but I had zero doubt Rider Huntington would crash and burn if he attempted to stand up to the former CIA agent. As far as I knew, Lloyd Mitchem could take the punk out in any number of ways without breaking a sweat.

"Cherise will be here in due time," I said. "For now, let him make a fool of himself." As he was at that second, dancing with Joslyn, his over-exaggerated motions a giant LOOK AT ME flag waving over his head.

Lloyd nodded and left me to it. I smiled at Brin as she hurried toward the table where I stood, the young woman bobbing a nod as she delivered more food, but didn't stop to chat, rushing off again, keeping her head down, jumping a little when Rider's laugh barked over the sound of the music.

Definitely something between them. Did I need to worry what?

It broke my heart to see my daughter hovering, nothing like her normal self, expression hurt and withdrawn while, still embracing the new her, Thalia swept her way through the partygoers with a huge smile and that odd head tilt that had me biting my lower lip in concern.

I held off searching symptoms on my phone, but I couldn't help running through mental health diagnosis in my head, discarding theory after supposition after guess as the night went on.

It was pretty clear to me Joslyn took great pleasure in tormenting my daughter, however. You have no idea the amount of restraint it took to keep me from bulldozing my way across the dancefloor and physically removing the nasty piece of work from the house for good. I didn't hear what Rider's companion said to Calliope, but I didn't have to. The flinching fury on my kid's face, the way she snapped back and turned away only to see her face fall into despair broke my heart over and over again.

Two things keeping me in place. Knowing Cherise was on her way and that Joslyn Precious might get the chance to be removed in handcuffs had a nice fantasy image to it I could really sink my teeth into. The second was the assurance if I tried to interfere Calliope would never speak to me again because if she'd been in a froth before over Thalia?

Yeah. That was nothing compared to her present state of mind.

It hurt me the most, however, to see Thalia witness the constant nastiness and ignore it. If there wasn't anything wrong with her? If she had simply become the woman she was supposed to be all along? She was far too Vestervillian for my liking now, thank you very much, and breaking up with Calliope would be a blessing. Not right away, I knew, but there was no way I'd ever encourage my kid to stay with Thalia if she was turning into her Uncle Chairman or Aunt Eleanor.

Yikes, the Vesterville curse might be real after all.

I did finally leave my spot when Rider approached Thalia, hand out. Calliope's instant move to put herself between them jerked me into action, and though it took me a few seconds to reach them, the fight was far from over when I got there.

"—her alone," Calliope was saying, voice low and humming with rage, her head down, hands clenched at her sides like she was ready to take him on then and there.

"I only asked for a dance," Rider said in that silkily smarmy way of his. "No harm in that, is there?"

Apparently, my daughter disagreed, but before I could circle Lawson and gently rein her in, she stepped into Rider's space with her face tilted up to his, almost chest-bumping him in her aggressiveness.

"I said, leave her alone," she snarled. "I mean it, Rider. Why don't you take your little friends and get out of our house?"

He opened his mouth to answer but didn't get to. Because Thalia spoke for him and, in the coldest and most dismissive tone I'd ever heard, tore my daughter's heart out of her chest.

"*Our* house," she said, eyebrow arching as she looked down at Calliope. "My house. I just let you live here."

Silence. I couldn't breathe, couldn't speak, should have intervened, but my chest was tight and there were no words. I stood frozen, a scream building inside me as Joslyn snorted.

"You heard her," she said to my pale and shaking kid. "You're the one who should pack up and go. Looks like she's tired of you finally."

I reached for her, but she was already striding past me, not running, my brave and powerful daughter, with her head high but leaving just the same.

Not me. You better believe not me. I closed the distance to Thalia, cutting Rider off, staring her in the eyes, a mere inch from her as I showed her just what I thought of her behavior. And watched as the color drained from her already pale face, the regret and shame that replaced her disdain, her blue eyes trying to evade mine while I refused to let her look away.

I didn't say anything. I didn't have to. Instead, I spun and went after Calliope, leaving Thalia to dance with Rider or not. I no longer cared what she did.

Oh, and if that Joslyn made one comment, one single remark? They would never find her body. Vesterville's grounds might not have been home, but I knew of a compost pile where she'd nicely decompose to dust.

I caught sight of Layla and her friends arriving but didn't have time to stop and talk to Cherise's daughter when my own needed me. Though she had a head start, I spotted Calliope exiting the side door to the gardens and followed, hurrying to catch up. When I emerged into the dark evening, I just glimpsed her bobbing black feather disappearing into the shrubbery maze that was part of the estate grounds, and though I knew it was probably a lost cause, went after her anyway.

I was immediately lost, pausing now and then to try to get my bearings. Didn't help I caught myself jumping and squeaking (okay, screaming like a little girl) at the occasional animatronic spook or clown or man with a chainsaw that had been seeded through the dark and towering shrubbery. Frustrated at one point, I paused at a crossroads, pulling out my phone, ready to text Calliope instead. Motion to my right had me turning my head, the surprising figure of Rider Huntington, his own phone alight, long strides carrying him with confidence toward the turn ahead, making me wonder. What was he doing out here? With no answer from my daughter, I carried on, bumping into Layla and her friends briefly as they giggled their breathless way past a black-hooded figure with a scythe, snapping selfies with the incredibly realistic prop before she waved and carried on.

I considered interfering, telling her to call her mother, but it was obvious by the way she avoided stopping to talk she was well aware Cherise wasn't happy with her attending the party and that I was a likely source of her mother's wrath.

Instead, knowing she was safe enough with her friends, I moved on, not sure now I'd ever find Calliope or my way out. I'd stopped at another juncture when Joslyn came strolling by, pausing to laugh at a decapitated corpse while I slipped past her. I wasn't above avoiding her, to the contrary. I was far too angry to deal with her right now but our conversation would happen at some point, make no mistake and she would regret ever being mean to my kid.

As I rounded a bend, I spotted Brin up ahead, but she was gone by the time I reached the corner, three possible paths meaning I'd have to be very lucky to find her. Same with Lawson who had stopped and was staring at something—likely his phone—before he hurried away. I have to admit, I was beginning to get a little creeped out, though the occasional encounters with small groups of partygoers helped somewhat. It wasn't until I turned a corner and almost ran face-first into Melanie that I finally did laugh out the tension that had been growing while she squeaked her surprise, clutching at me to gain her balance.

"Have you seen Brin?" No hello, Persephone, no how are you enjoying the party. Just that nervous question that had me thinking about her daughter's reaction to Rider—and her own, for that matter—all over again.

"I've seen a lot of people," I said, trying for levity but she wasn't interested, clearly distracted and anxious. Was she still taking her medication?

"Thank you," she said, hurrying on while I watched her go and shook my head.

I glanced at my phone, 10:27PM blinking to life. Great, I'd been in here almost a half hour already and nada. Maybe it was time to find my way out and let Calliope come to me. Thing was if I couldn't find her, the exit wasn't going to be any easier to locate, was it?

To my surprise, when I made my next choice in turns, I emerged suddenly into a large, open lawn, the center of the maze decorated with straw bales and fake torches, a tall cross in the center of the space just the height of the shrubbery hung with a scarecrow. And, standing under that scarecrow, was a pirate.

Finally.

Though, when I approached her, my focus on her, I realized she was trembling and when I reached Calliope's side, her eyes were huge, staring, her mouth open in a wide O of shock.

I noticed the body on the ground first. Wait, not a real body, but a straw-laden and flannel-wearing dummy. The scarecrow. But, if that was on the ground, what was—

Oh, no. I looked up, caught my breath. Realized the truth.

No scarecrow, though he'd been stuffed with enough ego and hot air to count. No longer, however. His empty eyes unblinking and suited body strapped, arms stretched out at his sides, to the cross, it appeared Rider Huntington had sold his last batch of drugs.

CHAPTER SEVEN

The fight between Cherise and her daughter wasn't pretty, but I kept my distance so at least I didn't get to hear what they said to one another. Like the conversations between Joslyn and Calliope, however, it was pretty clear neither of them was happy and there would be more words between them when they spoke again.

The end result, however, was inevitable as Layla, now loud enough to be heard as she left, shouted at her mother. "I can't believe you're treating me like this! I'm an adult!" Even as she sulkily followed a deputy out the door and, presumably, home.

Daughter problems all around tonight.

Mine—by blood—stood next to me in the foyer of Vesterville House, the remainder of the guests now sequestered to the ballroom under guard. I'd been hoping to keep the death of Rider Huntington hush-hush until the police arrived, my first move after regaining my wits the wise decision to text Cherise what happened. Unfortunately, I'd barely fired off my message, slipping my arm around Calliope's shoulders and turning her away from her continuing stare at the body, when a gaggle of partiers landed in the middle of the maze, giggling and tipsy, only to realize who it was hung on the cross at the same instant I lunged for them to stop them from looking up.

They didn't scream or run away or anything of the sort, though. To my continuing shock (I'd need an electrical charge to the heart any second now if this kept up) instead of crying and reacting like human beings, they all headed directly for the body with their cameras out.

If one more young woman took a selfie with Rider's corpse (#deadguy #DeadRider #Dider #Huntingdone #bestpartyever) and posted it to social media I was going to have heart failure.

At least Cherise acted quickly, she and several deputies landing on the estate within minutes, Lloyd providing her with a map for the maze, so she didn't have to wander around like I had. That meant she was in a position to put an end to the endless photographing session that only grew in magnitude as more people found the center, lured there almost en masse by the posts.

No one was screaming so there was that to be grateful for.

The sheriff managed to wrangle everyone back inside with her stern demeanor and a shake of her handcuffs, though I could see the clear disappointment in the eyes of the young people who were forced to retreat from the spectacle and really had to get a grip on myself. Horrifying, wasn't it, how social media had turned this kind of thing into a circus instead of a tragedy.

Okay, maybe tragedy was a stretch. We were talking about Rider Huntington. And yes, I knew how that sounded. But even he had a mom, right? A dad. Who hopefully loved him and would miss him. So, it was a tragedy for someone, even if only for Rider himself.

He'd have hated to see his picture posted when he looked less than his very best.

Cherise joined me, hugging Calliope briefly before sighing.

"That child," she said. Stopped. "Pictures. Of a *body*." She ground her teeth then shook her head. "She knows better."

Calliope leaned fully into me. "I'm so sorry

about this, Cherise," she said. Like this was my daughter's fault. "I knew he was going to make trouble. I just didn't know what kind of trouble."

"I'm going to need access to the party's social media event page," the sheriff told her while my daughter nodded. "Those pictures have to come down. Though now that they're out there…" she sighed again, tossing her hands. "No offense, kid, but what the heck is wrong with your generation?"

Calliope wiped at her nose, her cheeks, crying silently. "I wish I knew." She turned her head into me, hugged me then, sobbing a little. I hugged her back, Cherise wincing as I mouthed *Thalia*, the sheriff's face registering understanding.

I filled her in on what I knew while Calliope pulled herself together, the sheriff writing everything down. The only moment of distraction came when Owen Graves and the EMTs arrived, the town's young coroner already dressed in his white coverall and blue booties, the hood not yet pulled up but his gloves out and ready.

Cherise waved to him, Lloyd immediately stepping in to guide the team to the body. I knew deputies were already in the ballroom, questioning the guests, and was grateful

Cherise took a moment to be with us before she headed inside.

"What do you think you're doing?" Despite her previous behavior I was not expecting shrieking fury from the young owner of Vesterville House, Thalia storming through a pair of deputies and toward us, her rage focused on Cherise. "This is my house, Sheriff King," she snarled at the towering woman in khaki and black, a tall, thin wisp of a thing facing down a powerful warrior queen. I had no illusions about who would win and almost grabbed Thalia to distract her from confronting the sheriff. No luck, though. She circled around me, out of my reach, glaring at Cherise like this was her fault. "This is private property. Get out!"

To the sheriff's credit, she must have taken Thalia's recent oddness into account, as well as her prior experience with the young woman, because Cherise held her usual cool composure, responding with just enough sarcasm to cut through Thalia's rage. "You happen to have a dead body on your private property," the sheriff said, "in case you missed it, Ms. Vesterville," since Thalia chose to be so formal, "and I'm afraid that means your private property is now my domain. That is unless you have a guilty party to reveal so I can wrap up this murder case?"

Thalia spluttered, backed down. That head tilt reappeared, only this time she seemed distracted by something, looking away, frowning, shaking her head while her expression turned from furious to confused, dazed.

She looked up, met Calliope's guarded eyes. "Callie?" Thalia was trembling, hands covering her mouth a moment before she reached for my daughter. "What's going on? What happened?"

And there was a hospital visit in her very near future, while my daughter lunged for her girlfriend and hugged her.

"Lia." I barely heard Calliope's whisper, choking and thick. "Oh, Lia, something's wrong and we need to find out what."

Thalia seemed almost herself when she pulled away from Calliope, her blue eyes meeting mine, full of questions, full of fear and so lost I hugged her, too.

"I think I should go lie down." She pressed one shaking hand to her forehead. Looked up quickly, to Cherise. "Is that okay? Can I go lie down?"

The sheriff held her empathetic calm while she nodded to Thalia, one hand gently squeezing her shoulder. "I think that's a great idea, Lia." As soon as Thalia turned away, Cherise met my gaze with hers full of worry to match my own.

Like we needed this on top of murder, but you know what? Rider Huntington could wait. Thalia came first.

"Why are you just standing here wasting time?" How Joslyn had managed to evade the deputies I wasn't sure, but I did know her intervention wasn't welcome. Cherise turned to the ballroom doors with a frown, gesturing for one of her people to come to retrieve the escaped young woman, but she crossed her arms over her chest and shook her head in response to the attempt to corral her.

"My father is a powerful attorney in Bangor," she snapped. "You just try to make me go back in there, Sheriff King, and I'll have you up on wrongful confinement charges."

"And either you go back in there," Cherise told her in a mildly amused tone of voice that had to be the perfect weapon against someone like Joslyn because the young woman's face instantly settled into furious rebellion, "or I'll be calling your daddy and telling him to pick you up at county lockup. In the morning."

"On what charge?" Her pretentiousness was going to get her in more trouble than she could handle.

"Failing to cooperate in a murder investigation, for one," Cherise said. "Resisting arrest when you failed said cooperation might come next, but I'm still thinking about it."

Joslyn huffed then spun, vicious expression on her face. "Arrest her, then," she said, pointing at Calliope. "If anyone did it, it's Thalia's little puppy."

Okay. That was exactly enough of that. Except my tirade in defense of my daughter didn't happen. Calliope was far faster than me in her response and it wasn't words, oh no. To my dismay, she lunged for the other young woman with a fury and hate that I'd never seen on my daughter before, almost making contact.

Almost. If it hadn't been for Cherise, for the sheriff's excellent reflexes and obvious experience with such happenings, I was sure Calliope would be the one arrested. For assault. Because her fist?

No way it wouldn't have landed in Joslyn's face.

"There, you see? She's a psycho." Rider's companion stepped back, haughtiness as she looked down at Calliope only making things worse. My kid knew better than to struggle with the sheriff, but she looked like she wanted to. "Arrest her and let's get this over with."

"Thank you for your extensive investigative

insights," the sheriff said, no longer polite, harsh enough Joslyn blinked. "Now, are you going to county for the night, Miss…?"

"Connors," Joslyn said, chin rising. "Joslyn Connors."

"Miss Connors," Cherise went on. "Or are you going to behave yourself and go with the deputy?"

It was pretty clear which one the sheriff preferred and everything in her tone and demeanor suggested Joslyn comply.

"Fine," the young woman finally snapped. "But keep that," she jabbed a finger at Calliope," away from me." She spun then and marched back to the ballroom doors, past the deputy who tossed his hands in frustration at Cherise before following her.

As the sheriff looked down at Calliope with a grim expression. "I hear you found the body," she said. Paused. "Is there something you want to tell me, Callie?"

Oh, no, she did *not* just ask my kid if she killed Rider Huntington without coming out and asking.

CHAPTER EIGHT

I opened my mouth to protest, but Cherise looked up and met my eyes, her dark ones flat and rather angry. Which silenced me out of further shock because there was no way she thought Calliope did anything of the sort.

What was going on?

I instead found myself hugging Thalia who wavered there, eyes locked on Calliope, refusing to leave just yet though it was clear she wasn't well and needed to go upstairs to lie down. She clung to me regardless, though whether she understood what was happening or not I wasn't sure. Whatever was happening to Thalia, it would have to wait. Because thinking her trouble outweighed anything else actually took second seat to my kid being asked if she'd murdered someone.

No way, never in a million lifetimes. Even if that someone *was* Rider Huntington.

Wait, Persephone. Even if that someone was *Rider Huntington*?

Stop that. Immediately.

"I can't believe…" Calliope gaped in shock at Cherise before shaking her head. "I had nothing to do with it. I was in the maze, trying to…" she glanced at Thalia, then away, "thinking. I wanted to be alone." Oh, boy, the fight with Thalia and Rider prior to his death in the maze wasn't going to look good. She needed to stop talking, "I found him like that." She shrugged while I reached out and snagged her sleeve, pulling her toward me. With one arm supporting Thalia and the other in front of my daughter, keeping her slightly behind me and to my right, I met Cherise's eyes with my own and let her see just what I thought of this particular line of questioning.

"She's done talking without a lawyer," I said.

Enough.

"Seph." Cherise tsked softly, looking away before her gaze returned to mine. "I have to ask. You know I do. And according to Layla, Calliope and Rider got into it several times before his death. Am I wrong?"

"Lawyer," I said. "We're done here."

"I know how protective you are of Thalia." She shifted her focus to my daughter. "Callie, please. Just answer my questions so I can eliminate you as a…"

"Suspect," Calliope said, voice dull and flat. "You were going to say suspect, Cherise. You've known me since I was thirteen. I've been your daughter's friend for that long. Do you really think I'm capable of murder?"

"I think anyone is capable of anything," the sheriff said, sad but firm. "When someone they love is hurting or in trouble." Her dark eyes flickered to Thalia who shivered against me.

"Callie would never hurt anyone," she whispered. "Did someone get hurt somehow? Callie wouldn't do that, Cherise."

"Rider Huntington is dead," Cherise said, rather bluntly considering Thalia's condition. Where was her lovely compassion and empathy she was famous for? Did I even really know my friend and was she? My friend? Would a friend accuse your daughter of murder without proof?

"Considering you haven't even taken the time to investigate his death," I shot back, temper so hot I knew I wasn't in control of it but not caring, "maybe you should actually do your job before you throw around baseless accusations."

I caught the flash of her anger before

Cherise's face stiffened and she nodded. "I am investigating," she said. "And I haven't accused anyone. Yet." She closed her notebook with a snap, tucking it into her back pocket along with the pen she used. "Please see to it Thalia gets upstairs. I'll have more questions for both of you when she's resting." The sheriff turned and headed for the corridor under the stairs and the side exit to the garden, Lloyd appearing to guide her while I stood there, rigid and furious, hugging my girls to me until she was gone.

Don't think for a second this was over. Still raging, I spun on my daughter. "Take Thalia upstairs," I snapped. And strode off after Cherise to give her a piece of my mind.

Joslyn wasn't going to end up in county lockup tonight.

I was.

She had much longer legs than me, but I had a head of steam on, so I managed to stay just behind her and Lloyd and not get lost this time, though I didn't catch up with them until they stopped in the center of the maze where Owen and the EMTs had managed to lower the body to the ground and the coroner was performing his preliminary exam.

Lloyd caught the look on my face and immediately left me to whatever trouble I was about to get into, though I was sure it was more so his desire to go check on Thalia that had him hurrying away than my impending explosion.

Cherise turned and saw me, held out both hands in a gesture of peace while I filled my lungs and prepared to give it to her.

"Seph," she said, soft and low, leaning into me, that compassion finally showing up. "I'm sorry, okay? I know. But this is my job." The plea for understanding wasn't lost on me, just tempered by my anger.

"Callie wouldn't do that." I jabbed a finger at the cross without looking at it. "She would get angry, and she might hit him, but kill him? No way. Or hang him up like that."

Cherise took a long, quiet breath. "I'm sure you're right," she said. "But you also know over protectiveness can lead to passionate acts, Seph." Was she really trying to appeal to my logic right now? "Look, I'm sure Callie had nothing to do with it. Please, let me eliminate her so I can find out who actually did this." I shook my head, lips pressed tightly together. "Seph, I can make this official and take her to the office."

Over my freaking dead body, never mind Rider Huntington's.

"Cause of death was blunt force trauma to the head." We both turned in surprise to find Owen Graves standing there, looking back and forth between us. Clearly, he had no idea what he'd just interrupted, because he blinked a few times behind his glasses, pushing them into place with his index finger as he shrugged like it didn't matter and went on. "Looks like some kind of uneven weapon, maybe a chunk of rock or something rough." Weapon of opportunity? More than likely. "He was already dead when he was strung up." He half-turned, pointed to the cross. "There's a pully rig they used to hoist the scarecrow. Whoever killed him took advantage of it." Owen spun back. "No sign of the murder weapon, but I'll keep looking."

"The pullies," Cherise said. "Does that mean anyone of any strength or size could have hung the body?"

Owen thought about it a moment, then nodded. "Within limits, but yeah. I can't see why not." Great, so much for clearing Calliope that way. "I doubt they had gloves or anything on, though, so I'll test for DNA. The rope's pretty rough, so I should get a good sample as long as they didn't use something to protect their hands." Okay, that alone would exonerate my kid.

Until I groaned, remembering her telling me in excited glee how she'd helped the crew hang the scarecrow herself.

Her DNA was probably on that rope and

there was no way around it.

Except, I had a thought, because hadn't I seen him in here and didn't he seem like he was on a mission?

"Any sign of his phone?" If he had, in fact, been heading somewhere specific—let alone meeting someone specific—wasn't it likely that someone might have been the killer? It had been, what, a twenty-minute interval between watching him stride off and finding him hanging? Plenty of time to murder him and hang him from the cross.

Cherise didn't interrupt or try to stop Owen from answering, but he shook his head.

"No phone," he said. "I'll look out for that, too."

I told Cherise what I'd seen, hoping to distract her from our argument and Calliope, and while she took notes on the details, she didn't relent.

"Rider Huntington wasn't a maze for fun kind of guy," I said. "He's a long way from Bangor with no real explanation for why he crashed Thalia's party." At least she was listening, nodding. "Cherise, come on. He had to have been meeting his killer and that's who you need to be looking for."

"I'll look into all of it," she said. Took a breath. "You're not to work this case, Seph.

Understood? You might be an official member of the sheriff's department, but you are far too close to this." My own rebellion woke, but she didn't seem to care. "If you interfere and Calliope was involved," she hissed that at me, low and for my ears only, "you could both go to prison. Seph, I'm not kidding here. You poke your nose in and I'll arrest you myself."

So, it was going to be like that, then. Never mind I would never treat Layla this way, sheriff or not. I nodded abruptly and backed off, spinning and marching out of the maze, back toward the house. I don't know if it was my anger or the fact I'd now walked it twice but I found my way out without a problem, stopping on the threshold of the house when a text came through.

I'm on my way back from Dallas. Why was Trent messaging me? *Ready to take off now.*

Right, Calliope must have texted him. *I told Cherise she's not talking without a lawyer.*

Melanie needs a lawyer? What do you mean? Why? What? Melanie? *Is she okay? She didn't tell me she was in trouble.*

Head shake. *Not Melanie,* I sent. But before I could finish typing the next message, he answered.

Good, phew. Can you check on her and Brin? I know it's a big ask. They have to be upset.

Okay, this was the weirdest—and most frustrating—freaking conversation ever. *Thanks for worrying about your kid while you only think about your girlfriend and her daughter.* Could he read the snarl in my text? I hoped so.

Callie? Growl. *What's wrong with Callie?*

She found a body, Trent, I sent back, thumbs flying over the keyboard and to heck with the typos. *But yeah, she's fine and so is Thalia.* I wanted to add, *jerk,* but held off.

Barely.

I texted Callie but she won't answer. Yeah, sure you did. Not winning father of the year this year or any year ever. *I have to go, we're taking off. Seph, please.*

My least favorite word in the entire English language because it always seemed to be his favorite wasn't my first choice but all I could manage.

Whatever.

If he wanted more, he wasn't getting it. As for me, I had more important things to do than make Trent Garret happy. Except, now that I was thinking more clearly, hadn't both Brin and Melanie been upset to see Rider Huntington at the party?

If they'd set my daughter up for murder…

Trent was going to regret asking me to check in on them.

CHAPTER NINE

By the time I found the pair, I'd gotten over my huff about Trent's lack of caring for Calliope and refocused on the case. Yes, I know. Cherise told me to stay out of it. Thing was, I had information I needed to clarify before I could hand it over, didn't I?

I see you judging and tsking and shaking your head. Have fun with that.

My job, as I saw it, was to make sure Cherise had whatever she needed to find out who really killed Rider Huntington without appearing to actually uncover anything by being nosy. And since Trent had specifically asked me to check in on Melanie and Brin, me asking all my questions couldn't possibly be misconstrued as disobeying her because I was just doing my ex-husband a favor while clarifying certain things

I witnessed while making sure my daughter didn't go to prison for something she could never have done.

Excuses made and satisfactory to Momma Bear who growled her insistence I handle things at once, I went hunting with the intensity of a sharpshooter seeking prey.

Thing was, they weren't hard to find. A simple question aimed at Lloyd and I was heading for the kitchen where I spotted the two of them sitting at the giant center aisle in the uber-modern stainless-steel space filled with enough ovens and stovetops an army could have fed, well, an army from here.

Now, I know you already think I'm sneaky and that much was true, I had no qualms confessing to that fact. I didn't march right into the kitchen, no siree Bob. Why would I burst in on them when they were clearly already upset and cause more strain and conflict when I could loiter by the entry and listen in on their private conversation just in case either one of them was the murderer and confessed it to the other so I could leap, justified in my *ah-ha!* into their midst and save the day.

The fact Trent might have been dating— and harboring, Brin included—a murderer (or murderers, since they could have been in on it together) had me hesitating. He was, after all, an expert profiler in high demand around New England and even led his own team for goodness sakes, apprehending all sorts of truly horrific people who did terrible things to others on the regular. Except, love was weird and could blind us to truths we might resist seeing, right?

Hey. No pointing fingers. My daughter was innocent, and Momma Bear would fight you for even thinking it.

So why was I thinking the possibility was real in the deepest, darkest corners of my mind?

The trouble with eavesdropping was that often all you got to hear was anything but what you wanted to know. Brin's, "It's going to be okay, Mom," followed by Melanie's, "This is all so horrible," wasn't getting me anywhere. Impatient and wanting to get back to my kid before Cherise decided to go against my wishes and talk to her sans lawyer, I pushed the door open and forced a smile for the pair who looked up in startled surprise at my appearance.

Melanie tried to stand from the stool where she perched but Brin firmly pushed her down, confirming which of the two was the real mother in the family. Brin's stronger, more forceful nature clearly dominated her rather nervous mother which had me wondering what

Trent saw in her. She was almost my exact opposite.

Oh. Yeah. Okay then.

"Hey, Ms. Pringle," Brin said, hugging her mother who leaned into her. "The sheriff wanted us to stay put until she could talk to us. Is she almost ready?" She seemed more confident than nervous, despite her mother's state. I was already aware Melanie either didn't like me or was afraid of me (who, me?) and her need for anti-anxieties had me dismissing her worry. To a point.

"She's still at the scene," I said, coming to sit next to Melanie. "Trent texted. He's on a plane for home, but he wanted me to check in with you both and make sure you're doing okay." I had enough access to my empathy I was able to reach out and squeeze Melanie's hand. She responded in kind with a tremulous smile. "Rough night, huh?"

"For someone," Brin said, sarcasm pushed over into cynicism while her mother looked up with a little gasp.

"Brin," Melanie said.

"What?" She shrugged, still holding her mother like she needed to protect her from something. Me? Or the world at large? "Trent's kind to come home early."

I smiled again, grateful for the practiced

way I was able to settle into therapy mode and shunt off the emotions that really wanted control. "Is there anything I can do?"

"Tell the sheriff to hurry up," Brin muttered while Melanie shook her head, still clinging to my hand.

"Thank you, we're fine," she said. "We just want to pack up and go. Callie was sweet to ask us to cater this event. I feel just terribly how it's ended for her."

Tell me about it, though the fat lady had, as yet, to sing. "I couldn't help but notice both of you seemed upset by Rider Huntington's arrival." And it was immediately obvious I pushed too far, too fast, and should have hung back a bit longer because any chance Brin might have softened turned to rock-hard walls around her that she firmly slammed into place around her mother, too. Fake emerald eyes flat and no longer welcoming, she squeezed Melanie, not for comfort, I was sure, but for her silence.

"I don't know what you're talking about," Brin lied to my face.

"Melanie and Brin Anderson?" I turned as a deputy appeared, gesturing for the women to follow her. Which ended my opportunity, though you better believe I'd have another one down the road. After doing a little digging into the pair.

Melanie squeezed my hand one last time before standing and following the deputy, Brin hesitating on her way out.

"Leave my mother alone," she hissed, before striding off.

Well, that was a rapid turn-around from friendly and sarcastically chipper to bitter resentment. While I was well aware young women had the ability and propensity for mood swings, I knew there was more behind it than just ordinary angst.

Now, if only I could find out what without finding myself in cuffs, that would be peachy.

First line of investigation? The obvious. I messaged Trent, prodding him about Rider Huntington and if there was a connection to him and the Andersons. I knew he'd been at least peripherally involved the last time I'd encountered the trust fund dealer, so he had to have information that would help, right? Kicked myself internally when I remembered, after a huffing minute of no response, he was in the air and likely hadn't signed up for onboard Wi-Fi. Great. That meant waiting until he landed.

Forget that. I'd given up needing him a long time ago. The better choice? Finding a quiet place Cherise wouldn't think to look to do some digging.

The study was the perfect choice, though as I exited to head to the main part of the house, I felt a glimmer of guilt. Maybe I should be leaving this to Cherise. There was no way she would ever railroad Calliope, I was positive of that. She was too good and honest a cop. Besides, she had an excellent track record in catching the right people. Except all the murders she'd investigated recently? I'd been the unlucky one to stumble on the culprit while putting my life in danger to do it.

I should have been trusting Cherise to solve the case. Almost had myself convinced by the time I reached the foyer. Realized the deputies had released most of the guests and only a handful remained, including Joslyn Connors and Lawson Derrick. I spotted them as I passed the ballroom doors to peek inside the now open entry, noting they were arguing about something but not able to hear what. Joslyn abandoned him while he slunk off toward the food table and helped himself to one of the remaining drinks, Joslyn joining a pair of young women—oh, those beauty queens, seriously—their argument over but questions raised.

Did either of them have a reason to kill Rider? I'd not just seen Brin and Melanie in the maze (and hadn't Melanie seemed afraid when I'd encountered her?), but Joslyn and Lawson as well, and both had been on their own. Again, it wasn't like they were maze people. The idea Joslyn would willingly risk getting dirt on her heels had me snorting. So, what were they doing out there prior to Rider's death?

All excellent questions I wasn't allowed to pursue answers for.

Just my luck, Joslyn chose that moment to head in my direction, her visible distaste winning her zero empathy from me.

"Surely I'm allowed the ladies' room," she said like it was a huge inconvenience, and I was a servant or something.

"Of course," I said, my smile dead on my face. "This way." I turned and left her there, knowing she'd follow and, when I heard her heels on the floor behind me, decided Cherise could lock me up if she wanted but I wasn't going to stop asking questions after all. "I saw you in the maze," I said. "Alone. Get lost?"

"I don't have to answer your questions," she said, utterly dismissive as I paused by the door to the downstairs lavatory. She waited, lip twitching, while I blocked the way.

"I work with the sheriff's department," I said. Lied. Tonight, I was off duty, but she didn't know that.

"I don't care if you're FBI," she said.

I was positive she had some history with that organization considering Rider Huntington's favorite pastime. "Did you know your boyfriend was a drug dealer?"

She didn't bat an eye. "Prove it."

Yup, she knew all right. "You don't seem all that broken up by his death." Not that I expected her to be. Clearly a narcissist and the only person who could tolerate Rider (if he was paying, that was) for longer than ten minutes.

Her phone rang and she instantly fished it out of her bag, except it wasn't that one that was ringing. Her dark eyes met mine, flat stare threatening. "I'm not saying a word without my lawyer and Daddy is going to eat you for breakfast." She tossed her long, dark hair. "Out of the way."

It took everything I had not to smack her. Some parents really needed a crash course in teaching their brats manners. I did take a long moment to show her I wasn't hers to boss around, however, all the while the other phone in her bag rang and rang. Who needed two phones? And where was Rider's? If only I could search her purse…

I guess I stood my ground sufficiently she sighed.

"Fine, please get out of the way?" Oh my

God. She just made it worse.

I took two steps to the side, letting her pass. She jerked the door open and locked it behind her while I scowled at the floor and debated waiting for her. Finally strode off, positive she wouldn't be helpful anyway, so why torture myself?

Except, if that second phone had been Rider's, did that mean Joslyn had something to do with his death or had she simply found it and kept it for her own reasons? If she had motive, what was it? And would someone like her to whom a broken nail would mean an epic disaster even be capable of hoisting his body onto the cross?

Without help…

I needed to talk to Cherise.

Yeah, this was going to go well.

First things first, however. I needed to check in on my kids and, if the sheriff cleared her, get Thalia to a hospital for an evaluation.

But, when I made it to the suite, mind still spinning with possibilities, I heard voices inside and, unable to stop Momma Bear from roaring, strode into the room like I planned to tear it to shreds with my bare hands.

Cherise looked up from where she sat on the sitting room sofa with the girls, her kind expression turning grim while I stomped to a stop in front of her, teeth gritted.

"Lawyer," I snarled. "Or get out."

But Calliope was on her feet, grabbing my arm, tugging on me for my attention which she finally got. Growl.

"Mom," she said. "It's okay. Cherise has to ask. And there's a more important question." She looked down at Thalia who had been bundled inside a fluffy blanket, still looking dazed, disoriented. "Lia, it's time to come clean." Thalia's confusion only grew as my daughter let me go and faced down her girlfriend. "Was Rider here to sell you drugs?"

CHAPTER TEN

Thalia's reaction had me prepared to call 9-1-1. Like, right now. I was this close to ordering an immediate ambulance and a heavy dose of sedatives to boot. Because the moment Calliope asked that question, the Vesterville heiress leaped to her feet, tossing aside the blanket like it assaulted her. Worse, that head tilt returned with the little shake that always followed it as her temper returned with a vengeance.

"For the *last freaking time*," she screamed in Calliope's face, "I'm *not taking drugs!* Leave me alone!" Thalia ran from the room before either of us could stop her, slamming her way into their bedroom and audibly locking the door behind her with a heavy click.

I barely had time to register Thalia's nonverbal repetition of her demand for her privacy because the moment she disappeared, Calliope drew a long, shaking breath and then burst into tears. As she sank to the sofa again, she leaned into Cherise who, visibly startled by the show of trust despite the fact she'd been treating my daughter like a suspect, instantly acted in her usual kind and caring way. The sheriff wrapped her arms around my kid while I quickly joined them, sitting on the other side of Calliope, rubbing her back. Glad that she'd chosen Cherise for support because, frankly, it could only help her moving forward, the reminder she knew my daughter well enough to trust her back hopefully the end result.

All while regretting my little tantrum now but with no option to say so while my daughter wept her heart out on Cherise's shoulder. Which meant it was also a terrible time to offer up some information, right? Keeping my mouth shut was probably the better course of action in this particular time and place.

Except, as you have more than likely guessed by now, I was, as it turned out, the veritable Queen of Terrible Timing. Not surprised to hear that, right? Otherwise, you weren't paying attention, so shame on you.

"Before you start asking Callie more questions," I said, "you might want to ask

Joslyn Connors why she has two phones and find out if the other one is Rider's." Yes, that came out belligerent, despite our current attempt to soothe Calliope. I could have done better, just didn't manage to. It triggered the wrong response, naturally, Cherise glaring at me, though at least she didn't pull away from Calliope. Instead, she inhaled, but I shook my head at her before she could respond because I was far from done, thank you. Burning a bridge I'd built years ago seemed the logical way to go despite knowing better because I was still worked up and only human and a mom and, well. My temper was winning. "I wasn't being nosy," I snapped before she could reiterate her orders. "So, you can stop treating me like the enemy and listen." Yup, great tactic, perfecto. Just what she needed to ramp up her own resistance. All over the still shaking and crying form of my daughter, a wall between our mutual animosity. "Just so you know, all I did was showed her to the bathroom." Cherise relented ever so slightly because she was a way better person than me apparently. She even nodded, though her scowl remained, dark eyes narrowed. "And then there's Melanie and Brin Anderson," I said, not even thinking for a second what I was saying in front of my already traumatized and emotional daughter. "Both of them seem to have some kind of animosity toward Rider they won't talk about."

"Don't do that!" Calliope spun on me, fury on her face while I recoiled in surprise. She stood quickly, backing away from me, from Cherise, still crying, now almost hysterical while I reached for her. She slapped my hands away, furious. "Dad's happy, Mom, he loves Melanie and Brin, and you don't have the right to try to make them bad guys because you're jealous he's happy!" Wait, what? "Just stop, Mom!" She ran then, her logic painful to me because it held nothing of the sort.

Cherise sighed deeply while I stared after my kid and nursed the hurtful blow she just delivered.

"I have a feeling," she said very softly, "it's not your jealousy that's the problem, Seph." She met my eyes, that superpowered compassion worming its way through my anger and into my consciousness where a bell went off.

Calliope? Jealous of Melanie and Brin and Trent's happiness?

Her reluctance to talk about Melanie's daughter, of course. I'd read that as there was something wrong with her. And the fact Trent asked about them and not his own kid. Did she have reason to be jealous? Was Trent favoring his new family over her?

I'd kill him. After firmly beating myself up over missing the obvious.

Cherise stood, and I joined her. Hugged her impulsively and she embraced me back.

"I'm sorry," she said. Remember how I said she was a better person? She really was. "This sucks." She meant it, her anger present but Cherise doing her best not to let it ruin everything.

I really needed to trust her, but the Momma Bear inside me struggled to do so. The best I could manage was a nod against her shoulder. "It does," I said. Stepped back, sniffed, firmly reined in any response that might again trigger our mutual frustration. Was surprised when I succeeded. "I'm going to check on Thalia."

"And I have a few more people to question." Cherise hesitated a long moment before leaving as if she had more to say but just didn't know how. Thing was, I would have loved to hear it, honestly. To understand her mental process. Maybe it would have helped me to step back further and allow her to do her job without interfering. I simply couldn't reconcile her contemplating for a second the fact Calliope could easily have hurt Rider Huntington, struck him with a blunt object then strung him up for everyone to find.

She had a temper, of course, she did. She loved Thalia, without a doubt. She struggled with her girlfriend's mental health issues, absolutely. But murder someone in a fit of rage?

Um.

No, brain. No hesitation. My kid was innocent and that was all there was to it.

The thing was, I needed to be able to talk to Cherise, to share everything, instead of cherry-picking details to attack her with. Being on the other side of her support felt off, wrong, too painful to think about or linger over for long. Since I held back like she had, though, I let her go because I was worried if I tried to share, I might somehow do irreparable harm to our relationship by blurting the wrong thing. If these were normal circumstances, I wouldn't be so nervous. But this was Calliope's safety and freedom I was balancing in my head, not to mention Cherise and I had conflict in the past over cases when I'd overstepped. The fact she wanted me to carry on investigating with her (when my kid wasn't a suspect) said so much about the sheriff's amazingness I hated to think I might destroy the faith and trust I'd rebuilt on top of the mistakes I'd made.

Thing was my fear I might overshare myself out of that faith and trust may have already boarded a ship that sailed. But I couldn't think about it now. We were both grownups with jobs to do, my Mom job the most important right now even if she thought her sheriff one outweighed protecting my child. I'd deal with it after tempers had cooled, mine specifically. For now, a sick young woman needed my attention.

Dreading what I might find beyond the door but knowing I couldn't let her suffer, I went to the bedroom door and knocked.

It took her a moment, but she let me in, the sound of her approaching footfalls all the warning I got before the door unlocked and she opened it a crack. "Seph," she croaked like her throat was sore. "I don't want to talk right now."

"I know," I said as kindly as I could. "But Lia, I'm really worried."

One giant blue eye, now sunken and almost bruised beneath, met mine. "Me too," she whispered. Coughed softly. "I'm going to lie down. We'll talk in a little while, I promise. I'm just so tired."

It was a terrible idea, but I still had Calliope to save and letting Thalia sleep off whatever it was and regain a little strength might actually have been the best choice. I was wishing I'd brought Belladonna with me now and nodded.

"Please don't lock the door," I said. "I'll come back and check on you in a little while, okay?"

"Okay," she said quietly, fragile and tiny though she would have hated to know that wass how she appeared. "Thank you." Paused. "Seph?"

"Yes, sweet girl?" I choked up calling her that.

"I love you." She closed the door then, gone from my sight but never my heart while I leaned my forehead against the cool wood of the door and cried.

CHAPTER ELEVEN

It took a good ten minutes to pull myself together, helping myself to one of the other suites and the bathroom it hosted to blot at my damaged makeup, though by the time I was done I was satisfied it didn't look like I'd been crying, so I shrugged abruptly and accepted the outcome.

I headed back downstairs to find Calliope, a little guilty I hadn't done so immediately except, of course, I would have been a weepy mess and she needed someone to be strong for her right now. With my wits about me and my emotions under firm control (yeah, okay, right), I made it to the foyer with my chin up and shoulders back and didn't collapse into tears again.

My kid needed me, and I wasn't about to let

her down.

There was no sign of her in the ballroom and neither of the deputies watching the last dozen or so partygoers knew where Calliope had gone. I took note that Cherise was talking with Lawson, so at least she wasn't just fixating on my daughter. Okay, that wasn't fair, and I knew it but it had been a heck of a night so far and the last thing I'd expected from my sheriff friend was an accusation of murder.

Suggestion, Seph. And not even that, really, more a line of query that followed logic. But, to my overactive brain and heart, that amounted to locking my daughter up for life.

Overreaction much, Persephone?

There was no sign of Lloyd when I returned to the foyer, so I headed to the kitchen in search of the butler instead of wandering Vesterville House like some ghostly apparition in need of closure. I'd become accustomed enough to the warren of corridors nothing like the vast and palatial halls of the main house that I was able to make my way quickly and uneventfully back to the kitchen, though I admit to hunching my shoulders with some discomfort in the dimly lit, dark passages that made up the servant's area. Clearly whoever built this place cared not even a little for their staff, though I suppose, given what I knew of the history of the Vestervilles, that wasn't exactly surprising.

I rounded the last corner just before the kitchen entry and spotted, just up ahead, the last two people I expected to find together. Though Brin Anderson had an excellent reason to be back here, as far as I was concerned Joslyn Connors did not. Clearly, she'd been bullying the deputies again to win her freedom from the ballroom. Either that or Cherise had cut her loose. Regardless of her status, the fact she had traversed the less taken halls of the mansion in pursuit of Brin—or some other unknown purpose—had me pausing and attempting to listen.

They were far enough away only the hissing sound of their angry exchange made it to me, very clear from their mutual animosity neither was happy to be talking to the other. I considered interrupting, but before I could close the distance Joslyn tossed her head (her favorite, apparently) and strode away, huffing past me without acknowledging my presence. Pausing for one last verbal blow just past my shoulder.

"It's time you face the fact you were only ever comic relief," she said. "Have a nice life as a waitress." She walked off in a long but unhurried stride while I contemplated that insult. Obviously, Calliope wasn't her only target and Joslyn had a problem with other young women who she deemed beneath her. A clear sign of self-doubt, bullying behavior sourced in her need to be noticed and admired. While I understood her motivation, could logically categorize it, that didn't mean I had to accept it.

I could have gone after her but figured there was no point. Why waste my time on someone who refused to talk without her daddy present? Mind you, I could have manipulated her into telling me what she knew, I was sure, given enough time and space. Except I was supposed to be minding my own business so if I did manage to uncover anything, I'd have to tell Cherise and she wouldn't be happy with me.

Since our friendship was on a bit of an edge at the moment, I erred on the side of caution and chose instead to approach Brin who hugged herself with a furious and agonized expression on her face, tears dripping unhindered from her chin to the dark carpet.

"Here." I handed her some tissues I'd taken from the bathroom I'd used, knowing I would likely need them at some point. Brin took one with the barest lift of a grateful smile, blowing her nose after dabbing at the tears. "She's a piece of work."

Brin nodded, blew out a breath. "You have no idea," she said, voice thick. "Joslyn makes it her mission in life to hurt people as often and as deeply as possible."

"Does it help to know people like her only do so because they can't contain all the damage they are doing internally?" She looked up at that while I offered a sad smile. "If she's saying those things to you, imagine how horrible she's being to herself."

Brin thought about it a long second, then grinned like the sun coming up. "Thanks, Seph," she said. "That makes me feel a lot better."

I laughed. "It's supposed to make you feel empathy for her."

Not Brin, no way. She flashed me another smile, wickedly delighted and utterly devoid of compassion. "Anyone else," she said. "But never for Joslyn Connors." She sniffled then and I shared another tissue which she added to the first after putting it to good use. "Sorry, I know that sounds exceptionally shallow."

"Not at all," I said. "I can only assume you have a history, and not just with her. You used to be friends with Rider?"

Brin's hesitation wasn't just from anger, but fear, too. "Rider didn't have friends," she said.

"But yeah, when we lived in Bangor, I used to hang with them."

Interesting, and sadly made my mind turn toward what possible motive she could have to kill Rider Huntington because you better believe I was worried now she might be the person Cherise was looking for. "Was it hard to leave, move to Wallace?" Circumnavigating the obvious question felt like the right tactic and gained me a shrug.

"I guess," she said. "Mom thought it was a good idea, after—"

"Brin, honey." Melanie interrupted, exiting the kitchen door and rushing toward us, her arm going around her daughter as previously Brin had hugged her mother. The equally fearful flash in her eyes wasn't helping the case against the young woman any. Did even her mother think she could have killed Rider? I understood completely the irony of this particular situation, and don't for a second think otherwise. Here I was, a mother, trying to defend my daughter's innocence by flagging another woman's kid for murder. But the difference was I knew in my heart Calliope was innocent (yes, that little bitty nasty what if lingered, fair enough) while it appeared to me Melanie had her doubts.

Not my fault she thought her daughter

capable of murder.

"Excuse us, please, Persephone," Melanie said, guiding Brin to the kitchen door. "We still have clean up to do."

Again I could have followed and pressed the matter, but I hadn't as yet had a chance to look into the pair and there was the pending response from Trent to come. If Brin was somehow involved in Rider's death, they weren't going anywhere just yet. And if it turned out Brin was guilty, I had no doubt, in love or not, Trent would be the first to pursue them if they decided to run.

Think about how sad that scenario would turn out to be for a second. I was a horrible person to go there, right? Hey, you came with me.

No judging.

My subsequent search for my daughter turned up squat, though I did note, as I exited the side door heading toward the maze, Lawson Derrick had been given the freedom to sit outside on the steps where he quietly helped himself to what looked like a brand-new bottle of gin.

I sat next to him, hands in my lap, silent and calm, hoping he wouldn't leave. Was rewarded with the turn of his head, a brief nod, and, to my surprise, an offer of the bottle. Which I took, a small drink all I'd allow myself—I preferred my gin mixed, though the lime-flavored brand it was an expensive label and very delicious on its own—before handing it back.

That gesture of comradery accepted seemed to satisfy him, Lawson taking another swig from the bottle, elbows on his knees, staring with sadness at the entry to the maze. "I didn't even want to come tonight," he said. "Rider said he was going to come alone. Then Jos suggests we make an evening of it, and I couldn't say no." Something—it looked like anger, but not quite—crossed his face. Hard to read from profile. He looked down at the bottle in his hands, fisting the neck of it with one and cupping the bottom with the other. "I knew I should have stayed in Bangor."

"You've been friends a long time?" I took the bottle from him, had another sip. That seemed to loosen him up further as he nodded and sighed.

"Since we were kids," he said. "We went to the same private school. Only Rider was there because his dad's rich and I was on a scholarship." He squinted up at the full moon. "We got in a lot of trouble together. I could never say no to him."

"I'm sure he was very persuasive," I handed

the bottle back. "No regrets?"

Lawson met my eyes, grinned. "So many," he said, taking a drink. "My parents tried so many times to talk me out of hanging with Rider. They hated him." Lawson's shoulders twitched inside his dress jacket, face falling into that same odd expression that wasn't quite temperamental, but I still struggled to identify. "I never listened." He rubbed at his face with one hand. "Why didn't I listen?"

"Because they are your parents," I said. "Trust me, I get it."

He nodded. "I guess."

"What about Joslyn Connors?" She might not be willing to talk, but Lawson's lips were loose enough, perhaps because of the gin and perhaps because he was a genuinely nice guy who fell in with the wrong people and didn't know how to get out.

His whole being shifted, from weariness to sudden focus, though softened instead of intent which told me far more than his words did.

"She's better than both of us," he said, confirming what I'd just gleaned, that he was in love with her despite her preference for Rider and that would have only led to disaster in the end.

Except Rider was dead. Could that have

been the motive? I struggled to believe it, but people had died for less than unrequited love, right?

"I think you're undervaluing yourself, Lawson," I said as gently as possible.

He met my eyes then, his open and hurt, almost like a child looking for someone to soothe him after he skinned his knee. "You really think so?"

I nodded immediately. "I've met Rider before," I said, knowing I was walking a line but taking the chance anyway. "I was surprised to see him with Joslyn. His last girlfriend certainly wasn't from money."

Lawson nodded heavily, unsurprised and reacting with resignation, not resistance. "He liked girls to worship him," he said, voice very low. "He'd take some poor chick off the street or out of a bar and make her into a princess for a little while. Before using her to—" He flinched then, guilty expression undeniable. "Well, he was into some things that he never got caught for," Lawson said. "The girls he recruited usually went down for it instead."

Like a former waitress at The Blueberry Grill I knew. Not that Carlita Sanchez was without her own faults, mind you, but I knew the type well, so it wasn't all that surprising to hear Lawson say it.

"Joslyn was just a challenge to Rider," he said then, that anger returning. Definitely animosity about the relationship. But again, enough for Lawson to kill his best friend over? "He never appreciated her."

"Like you do?" I waited for him to answer, but that chance never came.

The moment he met my eyes again, sorrow there, Cherise appeared at the door.

"Mr. Derrick," she said, the slightest harshness in her tone aimed at me, no doubt. "Let's talk."

CHAPTER TWELVE

With no idea where Calliope had escaped to, I chose to step out of the sheriff's way for now and head to the study and the computer, as I'd planned earlier. It was apparent from Rider Huntington's social media he thought himself a celebrity, the ridiculousness of his personal profile's extreme extravagance almost revolting. Parties, women, yachts, private jets, you name it, he flaunted it, always with a gorgeous and scantily clad girl on his arm. There were any number with the pouty Joslyn Connors—her own social media was a blitz of duck-lipped selfies and petulance—while Lawson's focused more on sports, his rebuilt Mustang and a few photos with his parents, though he had enough comments, likes and shares of Joslyn's images I knew I wasn't off the mark in the least.

Still, no sign whatsoever of discord, at least outwardly. Which meant no proof to take to Cherise of my new and rather thin theory.

The possibility Joslyn killed Rider wouldn't leave me, though again motive wasn't really giving me joy. Yes, the two of them could have managed it, maybe, but so could Brin and Melanie for that fact, so just because Joslyn was an awful person didn't mean she murdered anyone.

Too bad. Would have been nice to see Cherise trade the arrogant little brat's sparkly bracelets for something a little more practical.

It was only by chance I stumbled on mention of Lawson being arrested, deep in Rider's social media. There was even a photo of the young man behind bars, his so-called best friend taking a laughing selfie of the two of them, the caption and hashtags completely unrepentant and horribly uncaring.

The bro be chillin' in the POPO clink, it read. #toldyounottogetcaughtbro #dudesuckerloser #servesyouright #begmetosaveyou.

Lovely friend, that Rider Huntington.

A scan of a newspaper in Bangor for around that time had Lawson arrested for drug possession, though a further update in the criminal column mentioned he'd been released due to lack of evidence. So, Rider had taken care of his friend after putting him in harm's way? I had no doubt he hadn't done so out of the goodness of his heart. More than likely, Rider had spent their entire lives together ensuring he had so much dirt on Lawson the young man would never be able to repay him or escape for fear of retaliation he might never recover from.

That sounded like Rider to me.

I did a quick check on Brin and Melanie, but there was nothing on the Andersons that I could find, in Bangor or otherwise, so I abandoned the search, sighing as I pushed back from the keyboard. Unable to just sit, my knees starting to jiggle in impatient energy, I stood and headed to the one place I might have been of assistance since I'd been banned from Cherise's side.

Thalia was still asleep when I tiptoed into her room. She'd discarded Abigail's jacket but was still dressed in her white shirt and skirt, stockings and shoes. I gently slid the clunky heels from her feet and tucked a blanket around her from the foot of the bed.

Then, with a massive surge of remorse and deep shame, I quietly searched her bedroom and bathroom for signs of a drug stash. When nothing turned up, I even went through her walk-in closet, finally closing the doors softly behind me.

She'd slept through the invasion of privacy, thank goodness, and though I'd have to live with the agony of that betrayal, I didn't regret it, not for a second. I now knew beyond a shadow of a doubt she wasn't taking anything. I almost wished she was. As I stood over her sleeping form, her quiet breathing through her open mouth making her look like the tiny preteen she'd been when we'd first met, I came very close to crying again. I couldn't help but go back to the first night she'd slept over, how I'd peeked in on the girls after they'd finally giggled themselves to sleep at one in the morning. How she'd looked like a waif, one of the Fay folk, a changeling and not human at all. Too delicate, too fragile and not much had changed as she'd grown. I sighed softly, clenching myself against the sadness of knowing there was something wrong with Thalia and I'd let it go on far too long.

No longer. As soon as Cherise wrapped up downstairs, I'd be waking the Vesterville heiress, and we'd be heading to the hospital. But it needed to wait until everyone was gone because there was no way I would add to her burden by giving her peers something to gossip about.

My phone buzzed, making me wince and hurry to the door, hoping the incoming message didn't wake her. Fortunately, she slumbered on while I slipped out into the sitting room and checked the text.

It was from Trent. He must have signed into the plane's Wi-Fi after all. Uncharacteristic of him and had me tensing all over again. *Rider Huntington was the victim? What was he doing there in the first place?*

I quickly fired off a short version of events. Didn't badger him about the fact he hadn't brought up Calliope *again*. I was far too interested in what he had to say about the murder victim at this point.

Because if Trent knew about Rider and Brin's connection and had information that could help Cherise—and possibly implicate the Andersons in his murder—he might have been preparing to hand it to me.

Except, as I stood there chewing my bottom lip, toes tapping in growing agitation, it was clear either Trent couldn't—oh, come on, Seph, *wouldn't*—answer. At least, not until he was able to do so in person because you better believe if he had something to clear Calliope, he was telling Cherise everything.

Even if I had to make him.

Okay, I was jumping to a giant conclusion

here. Trent loved Calliope, of course, he did. He was the most overprotective father I'd ever met. Came with the territory. So he wouldn't withhold anything that would keep her from a false sentence, I was sure of that. But if he was going to try to protect Melanie and Brin at the same time, he had another thing coming.

Like it or not, Calliope was his family, she came first, and his new girlfriend could just accept that.

At least now I knew for sure something was going on that went beyond Brin just hanging out with Rider and his crew. Wait, had she been one of the girls Lawson was talking about? Is that what Joslyn's comment had been about? If so, maybe Lawson could fill me in. All I needed was a fresh bottle of gin.

And to get him away from Cherise.

When I made it back downstairs, Cherise was questioning Brin. That had me more relieved than I expected, my body relaxing somewhat as I again checked the ballroom. The sheriff stood off to one side, head down with the young Anderson who had crossed her arms over her chest, belligerent expression on her face. It was impossible not to spot Melanie standing nearby, anxiety level so high she was trembling, eyes never leaving her daughter's face though a deputy stood in her way, separating her from her child. That was the big difference between us, I guess. I wouldn't have let a guy in a uniform (gun or no gun) keep me from my kid, thanks.

Now, who was judging?

I was surprised neither of them lawyered up, though maybe the frustration on Cherise's face meant Brin had? Movement further down the room had me glancing up, noting only a few people remained, Joslyn and Lawson among them. And, to another wave of relief, so was Calliope, though she kept her distance from those two, pirate hat long discarded, sitting in sullen silence in one of the tall antique chairs that lined the far wall, staring out a window into the garden.

My chance to talk to Lawson would have to wait until he was again separated from Joslyn, not to mention out from under Cherise's notice. But there was one other person I was perfectly justified in talking to (thanks, Trent) who I approached with a comforting smile while waving off the deputy. He gave us space without a moment's thought while I stepped close to Melanie and offered her a hug.

She took it gratefully, shaking so much I worried about her state of mind. Leaned back, now frowning in concern.

"Do you need to take your medication?" I

realized what I'd said the moment it left my mouth, hers falling open, eyes huge and full of hurt.

"How do you…?" She swallowed, looked away, hugging herself now, cutting me out. "How dare you invade my privacy like that."

Youch, too close for comfort, because my own kid accused me of the same thing. "I'm sorry," I said, keeping my voice down. "I found out by complete accident, Melanie. When we were investigating the murder in August, we needed to know who was taking Zexan." She twitched, shook her head. "I would never tell anyone. I'm just worried about you."

Melanie softened a little, sniffled, but didn't meet my eyes. "I'm not crazy."

I laughed sadly at that, and she looked up, clearly surprised. "Girl," I said, "we're all our own brand of crazy." She snorted a soft giggle. "I know a lot of people who could use a good dose of something on a regular basis." I eye-rolled while she relaxed the rest of the way, even her shaking diminishing somewhat. "I know it's wildly inappropriate, but there are ways to treat anxiety that have nothing to do with a pill." I reached out and squeezed her elbow gently. "If you ever want guidance—and no, you don't have to see me as a therapist, either—I can recommend some really great people for you to talk to that can help you get off Zexan. If that's what you want."

She blinked, tears rising. "Thank you," she whispered. "I'd like that. It's just been a tough year." She coughed softly, paled like she'd said too much.

"You left Bangor," I said, "because Brin was in trouble, didn't you?"

Melanie's tears fell harder, though she didn't sob, a silent and horrified fall of endless drops. Her lower lip trembled, face crumpling in grief. I tried to hug her again and though she resisted at first, she finally allowed me to comfort her.

But when she managed to pull herself under control, instead of talking further, she hurried off, head down, past her daughter who glared at me from where she still spoke with Cherise like I was going to regret making her mother cry.

Well, if she'd been the one who killed Rider? Brin would regret setting my daughter up for murder. Guess who I bet on to win that particular fight?

CHAPTER THIRTEEN

I hesitated to join Calliope, but finally caved to my mothering instincts and crossed to her, pulling up the seat next to her. She glanced my way and instantly hugged me before leaning back while continuing to hold my hand.

"I made a huge mess of everything," she whispered. "Tell me we can fix it."

"We're going to do our very best," I said, squeezing gently and refraining from pushing her curls back behind her ear because I caught Joslyn watching out of the corner of my eye and no way was I treating my twenty-two-year-old daughter like a kid and giving that revolting excuse for a human being even a scrap more fodder to throw at Calliope.

My whole "she's hurting herself worse on the inside" speech was real, but it didn't mean

I had to like her.

"Callie," I said, keeping my voice down, "did you know Brin used to hang with Rider?"

She nodded then, cheeks pinking. "I'm sorry," she said. "I know you're just trying to help, Mom. I didn't mean what I said about you being jealous." It was pretty obvious Cherise had been right and it was my kid who was feeling less than loved these days. Hopefully only by her father. Time to step up whether she liked it or not.

"We can talk about that later," I said. "Honey, do you know anything about the time she spent with Rider? Did she get into any trouble Cherise should know about?" Calliope hesitated. "You know how much I admire you for your protectiveness of others," I said, "and I'm well aware where you get it from." She grinned. "The thing is, though, sweetie, if Brin has history with Rider, it's going to come out one way or another and I'd rather Cherise heard it from us than from a police report."

She nodded then, sighed. "All I know is, her brother died. I have no idea if it's connected to Rider or not." Her brother? The death of a child would explain Melanie's use of Zexan. I couldn't imagine the agony of losing her son. Though, it now made perfect sense to me that there was an excellent chance Rider was absolutely connected to the other Anderson's death. Their reactions to his appearance could only mean so.

"What was his name?" I pulled out my phone as Calliope answered.

"Evan." She sat back, arms crossed, one pirate boot up on the next chair.

I did a quick check for his name but came up empty. "There's nothing about the death of an Evan Anderson in Bangor," I said.

"That's because his last name was Paris," Joslyn interrupted. She'd been eavesdropping, of course, she had. Now, yes, I was guilty of the same crime, thank you, but I did so to uncover truths and wrongdoing and she did it to be nosy, period. Still, her information was helpful despite my annoyance at her disdainful offering.

They must have used Anderson to distance themselves from his death. Which, when I typed in Evan Paris to the search engine, tagging it with Bangor, was probably an excellent idea. From a long string of arrests and one conviction that had him serve six months followed by community service, Melanie's son was hip-deep in Rider Huntington's pocket for what looked like several years, the abrupt beginning of his criminal career showing up near what the internet listed as his eighteenth birthday surely not the beginning. If his juvenile record was sealed, he could have been working with Rider since his early teens for all I knew.

A tragic life choice that ended a year ago with a fatal drug overdose at a party Rider hosted. No wonder Brin and Melanie hated him. And, if Rider had something to do with Evan's death—more so than he had by association, but a real and physical connection to the overdose—I could easily call that as powerful motive for murder.

Death delivered in a passioned blow followed by the humiliation of the hanging body? Sounded like revenge to me.

"Looks like the Andersons might have blamed Rider for Evan's death," I said.

"Oh, please." Joslyn again, that head toss getting on my nerves as she glared at me. "Evan got in over his head. He was pest and a hothead, and he couldn't keep his stupid little mouth shut. He overdosed, the fool." She turned away. "He had no one to blame but himself."

I thought I kind of disliked her before. I hadn't expected to learn to hate her guts.

Cherise had finally ended her conversation with Brin, the younger Anderson hurrying off with her head down. I waved for the sheriff to join us, showed her what I'd found while Cherise nodded.

"Trent texted me," she said, her back to Joslyn who was still trying to listen in. "Told me the whole story. He was the one who investigated Evan's death. His team was called in because Bangor PD knew Rider was involved and was being supplied out of state. But Trent said he never found any proof Evan overdosed on purpose, so they were forced to rule it an accident, and Rider got off because he claimed Evan brought the drugs to the party. Since Evan was the one with the record, the LEOs had to back off."

Rider was always a couple of steps ahead. Until he wasn't. Permanently.

"What did Brin say?" I winced a little, knowing what she'd said, but Cherise waved off my guilt.

"I'm sorry, Callie," she said to my daughter. "I know you didn't have anything to do with it. I'm pretty sure I know who did. Seph," she offered me a little, wry grin, "if you'd be so kind as to come back on the case, I could use your help."

I stood immediately, Calliope joining us. "Whatever you need, Cherise."

"Right now," she sighed heavily, "I need to go arrest two people for murder."

"But you let Brin go," Calliope said. "How do you know she and Melanie aren't running for the hills right now?"

Cherise smiled, sad but confident. "You learn a thing or two about interrogating family after being in this job a while," she said. "I let Brin go because I wanted to give her time to run to her mother and propose just that. While my deputies stand by to ensure they can't go anywhere." Clever and more than a bit diabolical but I couldn't fault her reasoning. "They'll work one another into a froth sufficiently by the time we get to the kitchen and tell them they're coming down to the station they'll be more willing to talk."

"I'm happy to help with that," I said. Paused. "Is Trent okay with this?" Melanie was his girlfriend, Brin her daughter.

Cherise nodded heavily, shrugging. "He's law enforcement, Seph," she said. "Told me to do what I had to." Of course, he did. "Ready?"

I followed her out of the ballroom and through the back halls, though was surprised to take a different route, emerging outside a few minutes later, in a small courtyard where a white service van had been parked in front of a single garage door. It stood open, two women hastily packing it with supplies, the rear entrance to the pantry, I now realized, for

III

deliveries and a catering van.

The narrow driveway wound down a hill through the trees, disappearing into the darkness and I now had no doubt a deputy or two in a cruiser sat at the end, waiting for the Andersons—or were they Parises?—to try to make an escape.

I had a moment of hesitation, wondering why they'd bother finish packing if they were guilty, only to defer to Cherise who interrupted them.

"Melanie," she said, voice deep and official, "Brin. I need the two of you to step away from the van, please. I have more questions I'd like to ask, and we're going to go down to the station to do it."

"You can't detain us." Melanie was shaking again, stepping in front of Brin who firmly moved her mother behind her in turn, glaring at the sheriff.

"We told you we want a lawyer," she said. "We're going home now, Sheriff King, and when we have one, we'll make an appointment to talk to you."

"That's not how this works, Brin," Cherise said. "A lawyer will be appointed to you if you can't afford one of your own. But you need to come with me right now or I'll have to charge you both with resisting arrest."

"We're under arrest?" Melanie sounded like she would burst into tears any second.

"You will be," Cherise said, "if you don't cooperate." She nodded to Brin. "I know about the assault charge," she said. "After your brother's death. You threatened Rider Huntington in public, Brin." She turned her attention to Melanie then. "And you sent three emails to him in the last nine months, all death threats. Do either of you deny it?"

Brin didn't respond, belligerence growing by the second, while Melanie looked at her daughter with a desperate horror that seemed ready to consume her.

"You both had reason to kill him," the sheriff went on. "And you were both in the maze at the time of death." Confirmed. "Look, I get it," she said, switching on that compassion of hers. "I understand the frustration, the need to get justice for Evan. Did you kill him together, or did one of you do it alone?"

Despite the confidence in Cherise's voice, I knew the sheriff was on thin ice pushing them like this, threatening them with arrest. She played a good game, I'd give her that. But any lawyer worth his salt would tell the two of them they didn't have to say a word or go with her if they didn't want to unless she did arrest them. And while she could have, yes, she really didn't have anything but circumstantial evidence, so they'd be out in twenty-four hours even without a lawyer.

But it was clear neither of them knew that, though the seemingly weaker of the two—had I underestimated her? Seemed that way—was the first to act in anxious response to Cherise's pressure. Melanie forced Brin aside one more time as she came forward, hands out.

"I did it," she blurted. "I killed Rider Huntington for murdering my son." And burst into tears.

CHAPTER FOURTEEN

"Mom!" Brin instantly grabbed her mother and spun her around to face her, horrified expression turning to desperation. Barely missing a beat, she then confronted Cherise, still clutching the shaking Melanie, her face settling into grim resolution so fast her previous reaction seemed like a glitch. "I did it," she said. Melanie moaned and shook her head, drawing a breath, about to deny it. Brin shot her mother a harsh, silencing look before returning that intensely bleak expression to the sheriff. "I killed him, and I have no regrets. I'd do it again if I could." She hesitated a bare second before gushing her next words. "And again, just to see him die." She swallowed hard, face contorting past anger and into satisfaction. "I don't care what you think of me, Sheriff

King, but I'm glad he's dead."

Her mother clearly disagreed. Melanie refused to let her daughter take the fall, her own words stumbling after her daughters, too late to stop Brin from trying to claim the deed while her face twisted to grief fed by fury. "Don't listen to her. She's lying to protect me, but I won't let her." Melanie sobbed through her words, almost unintelligible while she fought past her emotions to seize responsibility for the act. She finally jerked free of her daughter, voice a wail as she went on. "*I* did it. I acted alone, to avenge the death of my son." She barely managed to get those last two words out, choking on them. But she carried on with the kind of perseverance I never expected from her. I'd underestimated her own mothering instincts, apparently. "I swear to you, Brin had no idea what I had planned and had nothing to do with it."

"Stop lying, Mom, for God's sake." Brin snarled, grabbing her mother again, shaking her just a little, though her knuckles were white where she gripped Melanie's upper arms, so she clearly held herself back from the real force of her anger. "Just *stop* it. No one believes you. *I* did it and that's the truth." Whether it was the death grip on her biceps or her fading strength I wasn't sure, but Brin seemed to be having some success bullying her mother into weeping quietly, head down, shoulders around her ears. Melanie's courage and strength seemed to have drained away in the face of her daughter's conviction, protective instincts crushed by her grief. "It was me and Mom didn't know, okay?" She inhaled deeply, jaw setting as she let Melanie go, her mother sagging, no longer trying to fight. That seemed to satisfy Brin who fixed the sheriff with a steady look. "I saw him at the party and snapped. Followed him into the maze." She hugged herself then, pale and shaking. Did she wish Melanie's arms were around her? Her mother seemed incapable of action, frozen in her agony. "He deserved it, you know." Her chin lifted just a little. "He deserved to die for what he did to Evan. To the people who trusted him." Despite her resolution, her lower lip trembled, eyes filling with tears. "I didn't think about it. I just did it. And I'll pay for it. I'm okay with that." She finally glanced sideways at her mother. Was that regret on her face? Or something else?

Only one way to find out.

"How did you kill him?" I threw that question at her without thinking it through, since this really was Cherise's case. But the impulse to ask wouldn't be denied, nor were my instincts. Imagine my lack of surprise when

Brin stopped, stared at me open-mouthed, gaping before stammering then setting her jaw again.

Finally shook her head. "Just cuff me or whatever and let's get this over with." Which told me exactly what I needed to know. The fact she didn't, namely.

Okay, two things, neither of which were lost on me at the moment. First, they just provided one another with reasonable doubt and Cherise knew it, her flat expression meaning her immensely brilliant mind was seeking a way around this that didn't end in both of them walking if they were guilty. But that led to the second part of the equation.

The fact I now believed neither of them had anything to do with it and were, in truth, acting out of love for one another. Brin had no knowledge of Owen's findings, which meant she had no clue how he'd died. Thus, her hesitation. As for Melanie, while I fully understood the protective instincts she was right now in the grip of, she simply didn't have the courage to confront someone like Rider. And since it was clear to me the way Melanie rocked and moaned and Brin settled into acceptance but not guilt that they were only doing their best to protect one another from a crime neither committed.

"Brin," I said, while Cherise held off and let me talk, "your mother didn't kill Rider."

She flinched, face collapsing into terror and grief, verifying my hypothesis without having to say a word. Though she did speak, in a tremulous voice, almost like that of a little girl who was just emerging from a nightmare. "She didn't?"

That finally freed her mother from the shaking horror holding her rigid and condensed, unable to act until Brin's reaction cut her loose from whatever prison her mind built for her. Melanie let out a low cry, shaking her head at her daughter who sobbed herself and hugged her mother in a sudden rush of action that had them both rocking and swaying from the crushing impact of Brin's embrace.

"No, sweetheart," Melanie whispered, hoarse and graveled. "You thought I did?" She seemed dazed by that assumption. "How could you think I did?"

"I was sure…" Brin leaned back, mascara tracking down her pale cheeks. "I couldn't find you in the maze and then they found the body. Mom, you've said so many times if you got Rider alone, you'd kill him."

Melanie nodded, the energy she'd managed to muster quickly waning as she leaned into her daughter for strength. Brin didn't hesitate to lend hers, so this had to be the norm for them, a truth that saddened me. It was supposed to be the other way around, though if I lost Calliope to a tragedy, how much of my own strength would be gone with her light? No judging allowed, especially in the face of what they'd been through together. "I know," Melanie said. "But I never meant it, not really. Brin." Her eyes flew wide, her hands now clutching at her with her desperation showing before Melanie met my eyes, a shred of hope there.

While I nodded. "Melanie," I said. "Brin didn't kill Rider, either."

"Of course, I didn't," Brin said. Met her mother's wide and staring eyes. Had a moment of understanding. Before they hugged one another tight as the sheriff turned to me with her eyebrows arched.

"That's why they confessed," I said. "They each thought the other did it."

"And were just protecting one another," Cherise said. "Yes, I figured that out, Seph, thank you." She didn't sound so grateful, and I knew why. She'd just lost her two best suspects, though now I knew who to focus on.

My phone buzzed, a text from Calliope taking all my focus. Thalia's awake.

"I have to go inside," I told Cherise who

nodded.

"I'll deal with this mess," she said with enough sarcasm I knew she wasn't mad after all. "Thanks for the help."

I hurried back through the side door and into the corridors of the servant's quarters but instantly got lost. Somehow, I found myself instead emerging with a frustrated sigh to the right of the entry to the maze, tossing my hands before heading for the doorway I at least knew would take me back to the foyer. I was getting more than a little weary of Vesterville House, thank you, though all thoughts of Thalia and Calliope and irritation vanished at the sight of Lawson Derrick hurrying down the stairs toward the maze, glancing back over his shoulder—fortunately into the house and not in my direction—before carrying on at a heck of a clip.

My curiosity had a terrible habit of moving my feet without my permission and, witch boots or not, I'd spent enough time on the track jogging the last six months I was able to at least keep him in sight as he trotted his way deep into the shrubbery.

I almost didn't stop in time, tucking myself around a corner as he came to a halt and started scanning the ground around him. It was obvious to me he was looking for something, though what it was I could only guess at. Like, the murder weapon? Or Rider's phone, maybe? Or I was jumping to conclusions and the poor guy lost his wallet.

Except, after a short and audibly frustrating search—his language was not for the light of heart—he pulled out his own phone and dialed someone before speaking in an angry tone.

"It's not here," he snapped. "You're sure you saw it?" I only then realized he was heading back my way at a clip and had to force my body into the shrubbery, tucking tight against the harsh scratching of the twigs and branches, holding my breath while he stomped by, still talking. "It must have fallen. You don't understand, I need it. It has proof—" and then he was gone around a corner, his voice muffled and words undecipherable, but it didn't matter because he'd told me enough.

More than enough.

I texted Cherise quickly what I'd heard before hurrying to the spot where he'd stopped to examine the ground, doing my own thorough search using the flashlight app on my phone to cast light on the cobbled path and under the shrubbery. It was the only reason I spotted the small rock, round and dark gray but for the smear of red on the side and knew I'd found the killer.

Time to get a plastic bag and retrieve the murder weapon so Cherise could arrest Lawson for killing Rider Huntington.

I stood, switching off the light app, let out a satisfied breath.

As someone grabbed me from behind.

CHAPTER FIFTEEN

I mentioned my time in the gym, right? Well, I hadn't just been running or lifting weights like a boss (well, I had, so there). I'd taken Cherise's advice, chosen to put my safety ahead of my pride and signed up for a judo class. While the first few classes had been embarrassingly tough for someone who loved to appear competent from day one (guilty, okay? Get over it), I managed to corral my ego and actually learned a few things.

While I might not have been the expert my confidence craved just yet, if I'd learned anything from the last year it was that if I didn't figure out the best way to protect myself from those who didn't want to get caught for murder, I'd better do some official training into ways for a 5'3" (don't ask how much I weighed, so rude) woman to defend herself against someone bigger and heavier than me.

Case in point. The moment large, strong hands grasped my upper arms, I reacted, exactly as I'd been taught, had drilled into me by one of my patient and talented teachers who assured me instinct would kick in if I practiced enough. I'd have to hug Raeann when I saw her next because it turned out she knew what she was talking about (imagine that). Which meant rather than try to jerk free, an impossibility, I instead dropped into a crouch, forcing my attacker to follow me to lower ground, loosening his grip by changing the angle of his hold and his wrists before pushing off with as much power as I could with a forward trajectory, snapping his grip and allowing me to run like a rabbit.

Because self-defense class wasn't about fighting back. It was about getting free and running away to investigate another day.

I knew it was Lawson, didn't have to hear him bark a swear word when my tactic (thank you, Johnathan, hug also pending for my other judo teacher extraordinaire who made me practice on him over and over again) worked and I was suddenly free to do that running I mentioned. He had two choices, but instead of trying to destroy the evidence, he came after me, his feet thudding behind me, the sound of his heavy breathing getting closer. And while I was happy in one way he hadn't tampered with the evidence that would put him in prison for killing Rider, part of me wished he'd made that choice.

The panicked and frantic me who knew she couldn't outrun him forever.

I weaved as I heard him draw near, diving into an intersection, the sound of his feet skidding on the rocks as he corrected his direction giving me a little breathing room. But he'd catch me again, I knew, my desperate mind scrambling for what to do from here even as I stumbled into a shrieking witch whose broom she shook in my face, the animatronics' motion sensor picking up my presence.

I acted on instinct. Tore the broom from her hands while spinning in a circle, the heavy wood outstretched, just clearing the shrubbery and, in a near-perfect blow, catching Lawson Derrick across the cheekbone just as he lunged to close the distance between us.

I'd never seen anyone's eyes roll back in their head. No, wait. Calliope, once, when she was two and fell backward from a swing. That moment had been horrifying for another reason, my terror for her all-encompassing.

This time, when he groaned at the blow and collapsed where he stood, fear was instead traded for a powerful spike of glee that was fed, no doubt by hysteria.

That's how Cherise found me, standing over him with the broom in one hand, my fist on my other hip, half sobbing, half-laughing for my victory.

I stood off to the side, Cherise bagging the murder weapon, wishing I'd agreed to go back to the house instead of insisting on joining her in the return to the spot where Lawson either killed Rider or simply discarded the rock. I had a feeling this was the place, however, and tried not to think about the end result anymore.

I was so over Halloween at this point, though a silent thanks to the robot and her broom was not out of order. We witchy types had to stick together after all.

Yeah, I was in shock, sue me.

Deputies had already dragged Lawson out of the maze, so I knew I was safe, but it just didn't come through to my fight or flight just yet so when she straightened and accidentally dropped the bag, the rock striking the ground with a solid crack, I jumped.

Cherise winced, retrieving it again. "Sorry, Seph." She held her flashlight in the crook of her shoulder and neck and wrote something on the white box on the plastic with a black marker before tucking the evidence under one arm, retrieving the light with another and gesturing for me to go ahead of her. I instead fell in step, forcing myself to breathe while I filled her in on what happened, the first moment I was honestly capable of doing so. Had to stop talking a minute and blow my nose on the remains of the tissues I'd taken from the bathroom in order to be able to go on, especially at the point where I described the chase. When I was done, Cherise sighed.

"Woman, you're trying to give me heart failure." She reached over, trading her flashlight to her other hand and slipped her arm around my shoulders. "I really wish you'd stop putting yourself in danger like this." She was serious, too, no joking or amusement in her voice like other times when she'd teased me despite me knowing she was worried.

"Me too," I whispered. "I'm okay, honest. At least no one shot at me this time."

That was supposed to make her laugh. Fail.

"You want to know why I was so hard on

Calliope?" I nodded, frowning. Cherise tsked, let me go, stopped and faced me with the flashlight between us the only illumination, making shadows on her dark face. "Layla." She let out a low groan. "That girl… Seph, it's Callie this and Lia that all the time and I'm not angry." The sheriff shifted her weight from one foot to the other, visibly uncomfortable. "I'm just worried. She's leaving me, going to Australia and who knows where else in January and I know I have to let her go…" Cherise sniffed, went silent a moment. "I overreacted," she said. "When I thought Thalia might have something to do with Rider and then he was killed. Seph, I'm sorry, Calliope deserved better from me."

I hugged her, felt her embrace me with her own desperation back. "Why do they have to grow up?"

She nodded. "It sucks."

I laughed, Cherise laughed and we both sighed giant exhales at the same time.

"Let's get this wrapped up," Cherise said. "I need to go home and hug my kid."

Tell me about it.

Luckily, she still had the map on her phone (since the way I'd memorized was nowhere near here) so we managed to emerge into the side law a moment later. Found deputies had

Lawson, Melanie and Brin all waiting for us in the foyer, though when I turned to Cherise to question her reasoning for keeping the Andersons, she shook her head before I could.

"I'm clearing them both," she said, just as Brin spoke up, voice cracking.

"But it's my fault," she said. "I'm the reason Evan died. He wouldn't have even met Rider if it wasn't for me. Evan died because of me." And then she broke down at last, sagging into her mother, her guilt more than enough punishment.

Unlike Lawson Derrick, on the other hand. While a deputy led Melanie and Brin toward the kitchen to wrap up their night at last (how mundane a task, finishing packing the catering van after a murder investigation, so surreal), the other brought Rider's so-called best friend forward.

Any points he'd earned with me were long gone and though he seemed none the worse for wear for his short-lived unconsciousness, he glared at me with enough animosity I had no doubt here was the killer at last. And blurted what I'd figured out without considering the consequences.

"Joslyn," I said. "You murdered your best friend for a woman."

CHAPTER SIXTEEN

Lawson had the good sense not to argue, shrugging at the sight of the rock we now knew he'd used to strike Rider Huntington.

But rather than let the sheriff carry the investigation, I jumped in with my own questions. "I saw you looking for it," I said. "That's how I found it, Lawson." His dark eyes met mine, expressionless, lips a tight, white line as though he'd sealed them shut forever. "And I heard you on the phone. The question is, who were you talking to? And who were you working with?" No reply, just that dead stare. "Or were you looking for something else?" I took a giant risk, remembering Rider and I shared the same model and case and pulled my cell out of my back pocket. Saw his eyes widen in surprise and had my answer. "You were looking for Rider's phone," I said, wiggling mine in his direction. "Guess who found it?"

That hit the spot, and far easier than I expected. Lawson's attempt at rebellion caved into despair as he sobbed once, then shook his head, broad shoulders shaking while he tried to regain his emotional control.

"You don't understand," he said, choking on his words.

"So maybe explain it to us," Cherise said. "What possessed you to kill your best friend?"

Lawson's almost violent denial surprised both of us, the sheriff exchanging a look with me as he snarled and tried to shake off the deputy holding him in place, hands cuffed behind his back.

"Rider didn't have friends," he said, sullen and furious. "He had tools and weapons and people he manipulated, blackmailed into doing what he wanted." He coughed a harsh laugh. "Best friend? He owned me and has since we were teenagers."

Well now, this wasn't really a giant revelation, but it still surprised me. "Lawson," I said, "what did he do to you to make you obey him all this time?"

"It's what he convinced me to do," the young man said, his tone now turning to regret, to the ache of horror and old despair. "The first week I met Rider I thought he was amazing. He had tons of money, so he bought me stuff, took me with him when he snuck out of school. I would have done anything for him. He had this charm, this charismatic pull." Lawson sagged, no longer fighting the deputy's hold on him, something much bigger and more powerfully impactful way ahead of the man in uniform. "He drugged this kid at a party," he said, voice going dull, defeated. "The guy owed Rider money and he wanted it back. Except he had me do it, filmed the whole thing like it was a joke. I did it, never thought anything of it. Rider was my friend." His face twisted in self-hate and the kind of recrimination that could ruin you if you let it. Clearly, it had done so to Lawson. "I found out the next morning the dose Rider told me to give to the kid killed him." He swallowed hard, a little green. "I killed him." He drew a shaking breath before meeting my eyes, not asking for mercy or caring or compassion, just for someone to listen to a story he finally got to tell, one he'd been waiting to unload for years. "I went to Rider in a panic, terrified someone would find out. You know what he said?" I held my silence and space for him as he let out a nasty, painful laugh. "That he owned me now because he knew my secret. You know what else?" This time I shook my head. "He did it on purpose. I found out because he did it to others. He had me kill an innocent kid who never did anything to anyone, someone he saw as disposable, so he could control me." Lawson moaned softly, almost as if he couldn't bear what he'd endured for much longer. "And he was right. I was so afraid. There was nothing I could do. So, I did what I was told."

"You were part of his drug enterprise," Cherise said after giving him a moment to recover his composure.

He nodded at that. "I was his right hand," Lawson said. "I had myself convinced it was okay. Instead of fighting against it, I gave in to it, you know?" He sniffled, tried to wipe his nose on the shoulder of his jacket, failing thanks to his hands still pinned behind him. Bleary resignation seemed all that was left to him. "If you can't beat Rider, join him. I even told myself it was for my own good. I made a lot of money. But he hung that boy's death over my head every time I tried to do anything he didn't like. A constant reminder of what I'd done, who I'd become for him." He wept openly now, trembling lips parted. "I sold my soul to Rider Huntington and there was no way out."

"Lawson," I said. "Something happened to

make you fight back after all this time. What was it?"

He shuddered, resuming control again, then shrugged. "You were the catalyst," he said, nodding to me while my eyebrows shot up in surprise. "When you confronted Rider that day and suggested he might not be trustworthy in front of the gang bodyguards, they almost killed him for me." That would have been a blessing. Hey, I didn't mean it that way. But if Rider's partners had killed him in Bangor, I wouldn't be standing in the foyer of Vesterville House with a broken young man in front of me facing life in prison for murder. Happy now? And yes, I was glad Rider was dead, so there. "He agreed to pay them off and it worked. Except when his father found out he'd blown through his trust fund, he cut Rider down to a fraction of what he was accustomed to and, without the gangs to help him sell, he was suddenly broke."

Yeah, that would have gone over well. "I'm not sorry, Lawson," I said.

He actually managed a little smile. "Me either," he said. "Rider was too arrogant for his own good, and even though he was careful to make sure he had dirt on everyone around him and made them do the actual crimes, so he'd stay clean, he was going to eventually get caught, likely sooner rather than later. I heard there was an FBI agent investigating him, something to do with Evan Paris and his death." Well now. There was an excellent chance I knew exactly who said agent was and why he was digging into Rider. But that was for later.

"Rider killed Evan," Lawson said, quiet, an ache in his voice, this new reveal enough to silence my speculations about Trent. "He had to do it himself because no one would help. Evan's sister, Brin," he tossed his head toward the other end of the house where she and Melanie had been escorted, "wanted him out of Rider's control. He never managed to get anything on her, but he had lots on Evan. Tried to blackmail Brin, but she swore she'd have Evan agree to testify against Rider and make a deal for immunity. So, Rider panicked and killed him." Poor Brin and Melanie. "I realized then there was no way out but getting rid of Rider." Another shrug, this one casual, like he'd made a choice for lunch and wasn't sold on it, but he could live with it. "If he was willing to kill Evan, he was willing to do the same to all of us."

It sounded like he was working on his self-defense plea already, but I understood his motivation, at least. "Why wait this long?"

"I needed to figure out how to get him in a place he was vulnerable," Lawson said. "He's really careful, paranoid." He swallowed. "Was. I tried a couple of times over the last few months, but he kept loyal people around him, those who thought like I had, that they might as well do as he said and find a way to like it. So, I finally decided to set him up." He tilted his head toward the cell phone in my hand. "I sent an anonymous message about a week ago, pretending to be someone from another gang, looking for a new partner. Rider had been trying for ages to find someone to work with him again, but he'd never found anyone because of you." A little, almost hysterical chuckle escaped him. "He was so mad. But your ex-husband is FBI, and the sheriff is your friend… even he wasn't that deluded." He caught his breath as it hitched, then went on. "He jumped on the chance, went from sullen frustration and abusing everyone to king arrogant all over again. Didn't even question the offer. So maybe he was that deluded after all."

"You set up the meet for the party," I said. Smarter than the average Rider, apparently.

"It was neutral ground," Lawson said. "I suggested it to him when he was trying to figure out where to meet. He never suspected a thing."

Of course not. Lawson was, for all intents and purposes, his initial and most loyal victim. "When enough time passed and he'd had a few drinks, you messaged him again."

Lawson let out a long, slow breath. "I followed him into the maze after texting him he had to go alone. Caught up with him where you found that." Another nod, for the bloody rock. "He was furious. Thought I was going to blow the deal. Turned away from me." He sounded so amazed, dazed even. "He had no idea. I'd taken the rock with me, knew a gun would be traceable, a knife. Figured maybe I could make it look like a crime of passion, especially after I saw Brin here." He had the good grace to look a little guilty. "I was hoping her history with Rider would deflect from me and it did."

"It did," I said. "That's why you hung him up on the scarecrow's cross?"

He straightened, as though suddenly deciding to take full responsibility and face his fate with courage. I had to hand it to Lawson, he'd survived an ordeal and done some terrible things, but he wasn't going to let it break him. "I was looking for somewhere to hide the body," he said. "When I saw the cross it just… seemed to fit."

That still didn't answer the question of the hour, however. "Who were you talking to, Lawson?" I had a feeling I already knew because he'd come with one other person tonight, hadn't he? The thing I wanted to know, though, was she in on it or was Joslyn an innocent party?

He hesitated a long moment before Cherise prodded him again. "We can just check your phone," she said, gesturing for the deputy to hand her the plastic bag where he kept Lawson's cell.

The young man met my eyes, his own hopeless and I knew.

"Joslyn," he said. Sighed. "I lied about one thing." Just one? "I took credit for the plan but... this was all her idea."

CHAPTER SEVENTEEN

There was an excellent chance he was only trying to create his own reasonable doubt ruling but, as I held his gaze and saw his misery there, I knew he was telling the truth.

Besides, it would have taken a lot of convincing to have someone like Lawson—after years of servitude—turn on his master and the death of a young man, as horrible or not, was just another death in a long chain of them if he was to be believed. But if his feelings for Joslyn were manipulated, I could easily see him turning on Rider for her.

If she asked him to. Time for the real truth to come out.

"You don't understand," he blurted as Cherise reached for her phone, dialed and started whispering as she turned her back,

"Joslyn was worried about me." Sure, she was. "She came to me, she was terrified after Evan died that Rider was going to kill me, too. I watched him after that, saw how paranoid he was. She was right, no one was safe, least of all me." What horrors had she murmured to him in false concern, twisting his adoration into a weapon she used to murder Rider Huntington? But what purpose would she have to do so unless…

"What did Rider have on Joslyn, Lawson?" That was the only explanation behind her action as far as I could guess.

He flinched, shook his head, paling out, lips sealing again.

"We're going to find out, you know." Cherise said that gently as she hung up and tucked her phone away. "I've put out an APB on her, Lawson. She'll get picked up before she reaches Bangor."

"No, you don't see," he said, blurting again. "She didn't love him." That came out in a whisper. "She told me, she said she was only with him because she was afraid of him and that she wanted to be with me." Oh, you poor, poor boy. The classic lie of a femme fatale out for her own gain. "She said we could get rid of Rider, make it look like a gang hit and then take over his operation together." Ah, now the real motive, excellent. He didn't seem to notice he was digging them both a giant hole, rushing on with his heart on his sleeve and his naiveite visible despite everything he'd been through. Amazing he held onto any innocence and trust after years under Rider's thumb. Actually gave me hope for him in the future, as odd as that might sound. "With Rider out of the way we could have convinced his old partners to resume business." He blinked then, flushed. Did he realize he'd just confessed to carrying on old criminal activity? Didn't matter now. He was already going to prison for murder, so what was a little drug dealing between friends? "You found his phone," he said then, that dull despair returning. "He kept snippets of all the incriminating files on it, and the password to the cloud storage where the full ones are. All the films he made of criminal activity, all the blackmail material."

"That's why you needed his phone," I said. And now, so did we. What I really needed at the moment, however, was Joslyn and, like it or not, Lawson was about to give her to me. "You realize this is my phone." I showed him the lock screen, Calliope's smiling face, holding Belladonna in her arms, Thalia leaning in and waving. The young man blanched, panic rising, before he met my eyes with so much hurt, I realized the betrayal was more damaging than anything he'd expected. I felt sorry for him as I pushed on. "Lawson, you couldn't find Rider's phone because someone else has had it all along and never told you." He started shaking his head, crying again, knees buckling. "Joslyn has it," I said, with as much conviction as I could put in my voice. No proof, but that second ringing she refused to answer earlier? It had to be Rider's cell. Even if it wasn't, he didn't know that, right? "She's had it since Rider died and she kept it from you, Lawson. Why do you think that might be?"

He fish lipped, fought for breath past sobs while Cherise sighed.

"She didn't want to partner with you, Lawson," the sheriff said in her kindest voice. "She planned to own you like Rider did."

If we could have crushed him any further, I really don't know how we would have accomplished it. The deputy had to struggle to keep Lawson on his feet, his wailing turning to a groaning realization that ended in acceptance so deeply damaging I knew we'd finally erased any of the innocence he'd maintained despite himself.

Way to be the end to this young man's last thread of himself, Seph.

"We need that phone," Cherise spoke low

and tense as she turned to me, the deputy wrestling Lawson into a chair before he could fall to his knees, standing over the young man who sobbed his heart out. "Why did I let her go?"

"Not your fault," I said. "She didn't kill him, and without knowing about the phone's contents, there was no reason to keep her. Did you ask her about it?"

Cherise nodded. "Even let me search her purse," she said. "There was only one phone, Seph. Are you sure she had it?"

Now, I wasn't so, but it made sense, so I carried on. "Maybe she stashed it somewhere," I said. Had an epiphany and was already moving as I said, "the bathroom!"

It made sense she'd hide it there. But after a brief search, we turned up nothing.

"She knew I noted the second ringing," I said, leaning over the sink while Cherise stripped off her blue gloves and dumped them in the trash she'd just sifted through. "She likely stashed it in here, talked to you then came back and retrieved it." Crappy.

"I'm going to coordinate with the state police," Cherise said. "I'll take Lawson to the station then get out there and help in the search." She squeezed my shoulder. "We'll find her. And she'll pay for her part in this."

I watched her go, Lawson with his head down, making no move to struggle against the cuffs or her firm grip on his arm, all the fight gone out of him at last.

Such a shame and a wretched way to end a young life. Sure, he was going to prison, so he wasn't dying or anything, but in trusting someone he never should have put his faith in, Lawson's choices led him ultimately to murder and the rest of his life behind bars.

What a waste.

It wasn't until Lloyd closed the door and joined me, I realized I hadn't yet gone upstairs to see Calliope and Thalia. A little guilty the investigation got in the way, I hugged him, to his immense surprise, though after he stiffened initially, he hugged me back with real warmth.

"I'm going to check on the girls," I said when I let him go, surprised to find his eyes moist and that he had to clear his throat before speaking.

"Of course, Ms. Pringle," he said. "I'll see to the Andersons." Lloyd strode away at a clip a man half his age would envy, shoulders back, head high, while I grinned after him.

Maybe I made his night.

It was hard to focus as I climbed the stairs to the third floor, mind turning over all the details of the case and the worry that Cherise, despite her optimism, would never find Joslyn Connors. Though, there was every reason she'd just run home to Daddy, right? If that was the case, while maybe she might fight it in court, if she had Rider's phone in her possession when she was taken into custody, that would be enough evidence to prove she was involved.

Yes, she could claim Rider gave it to her and she had no idea what was on it, but I was holding onto the hope that Lawson's reaction to my question—what did that creep Rider have on Joslyn—was buried somewhere in that cell phone, too.

She would at least go down for whatever it was she'd done Rider had caught on film, even if not for aiding and abetting (and cheering on) Lawson's penchant for murder.

The hallway lights had been dimmed, though I barely noticed, but when I reached the main suite door, I realized there was no illumination coming from inside. Darn it, did the girls go downstairs and I climbed my weary bones all the freaking way up here for no reason? Well, I was here, so I might as well check, right?

The moment I opened the door, I realized two things. The girls hadn't gone down yet, and they had oddly chosen to huddle on the sofa near the fireplace, a single light from a small lamp in the bedroom beyond the only glow. Now, snuggling wasn't a bad idea in Thalia's case, since she could use all the love and support we could give her now. But the looks on their faces as I entered the room and paused a few steps inside while they stared at me, eyes huge, Calliope biting her lower lip, seemed, well.

Scared.

"Nice of you to join us," Joslyn Connors said in a low and menacing tone as the door slammed behind me. I spun to find her facing me, a gun in her hand. "Go sit down and shut up."

Great. Just when I thought I wouldn't get shot at today.

CHAPTER EIGHTEEN

"Lawson told us everything." Best in cases like this to lead with the strongest truth, see if I could shake her. "I know you killed Rider."

Joslyn barely flinched. "Correction, Lawson killed Rider because Rider had proof Lawson murdered someone when they were fourteen." She shrugged. "I was just so worried about Lawson," her tone changed entirely, softening out, turning almost sweet and caring, trembling just enough it sounded like she was near to tears when I knew she was nothing of the sort. Well, real tears, at least. I doubted she'd cried over anyone but herself her entire life. "I heard Rider threatening to hurt him, but I had no idea he'd *kill* him." She paused in her little performance, another artful shrug of her narrow shoulders ending the show. "Daddy will put me on the stand and that will be that."

"You orchestrated the whole thing," I said. "And when we get access to Rider's cloud storage and show a judge what you did, Joslyn, you'll be going away for murder yourself, as well as conspiracy to commit. Hope you like orange and roommates."

Joslyn snarled at me. "You found it," she said. "Give it to me."

Wait, what? "Cherise has it," I said. "Sorry about that."

A tiny, petulant shriek escaped her, almost adorable, really, except for the hate and rage in her eyes and the way her hand now shook, the gun wobbling just a little. "You idiot," she snarled.

"I told you I didn't have it," Calliope said, sullen enough to draw Joslyn's focus while I turned and hissed at my daughter to be still. She ignored me, standing, leaving Thalia weak and limp on the sofa, my brave, foolish kid putting herself between the gun and her true love. "You didn't have to threaten us. I never had Rider's phone."

Joslyn's tsk of frustration was clearly indecision. Which meant an opening.

"Put the gun down," I said. "It's too late, Joslyn." While my mind scrambled. Who had Rider's phone? Who found it? I tried to think if I'd noticed someone else going into the bathroom, but honestly, so many things had happened since I'd left her there, I couldn't recall a single detail. The fact remained, someone took it and that meant there was still a chance to find it. "You're only making matters worse for yourself."

It was obvious things weren't going the way the princess planned and she wasn't sure what to do about it. I watched desperation chase fury after panic after rage until she finally seemed to make up her mind, hand steadying, face flattening into grim aggression.

"Get her up." She waved the gun at Calliope and Thalia. "I said, get her *up*. Now."

I watched my daughter rebel a long moment before she finally complied, though she did her best to turn her body as she guided Thalia to her feet, using herself as the best shield she could.

"Join your mother." Joslyn chewed her lower lip with enough force, her gaze darting to the door, I was pretty sure what she had planned. Calliope and Thalia slid in beside me and, taking a page from my kid's book, I slid my arm around the weak Vesterville while positioning myself in front of her the best I could. The gratitude in Calliope's eyes made me teary.

We were going to make it out of this and get Thalia to the hospital and see Joslyn in prison for what she'd done. What she was doing.

Momma Bear promised.

"You three," Joslyn snarled, circling away from us, gesturing to the exit, "are going to walk me out of here and to my car. Move it." She took a moment to glare right at me. "No smart ideas. I will shoot you."

"I've been shot before," I shrugged. "Stop threatening us and let's just go already." Calliope's huge, hazel eyes stared at me in utter horror before she grinned.

At least one of us believe everything was going to be okay. I wished I had her faith in me, but I was behind the false bravado, so it was hard to hide from the fraud for long.

Didn't matter. Let Joslyn escape. Again, I was sure she'd run to Daddy which meant Cherise and the state police would be right behind her and since she didn't have Rider's phone, she had no way of covering up what she'd done.

She'd get hers one way or another. Doing the smart thing and letting her go meant nothing in the long run and I didn't feel the need to play hero again tonight.

Then again, as we entered the dim hallway,

Joslyn behind us, I wouldn't put it past her to shoot us anyway. The fact we were heading downstairs, however, meant Lloyd and his particular skill set would be in play, so I could only hope he'd make a surprise appearance and save the day.

No such luck, apparently. Calliope led us, instead of to the main staircase, through a narrow door and down a spiral set of steps to the main floor, a back way to the ground level I didn't even know existed. The doorway at the bottom let us out into the garden on the front right side of the main wing, no lights save for the main ones over the circular drive illuminating the darkness.

"This way." Calliope led, still with Thalia in her arms, and I followed, putting myself between them and the gun, though my shoulders twitched, and my heart sped up (further, sped up *further* because you better believe it was pounding) at the anticipation the sociopath following me could pull the trigger at any moment.

"You must have thought you were so smart." Joslyn hissed that at me, almost in my ear and I jumped, not realizing she was right on my heels until she spoke. The muzzle of the gun poked me in the lower back, and it took everything I had not to squeak my terror, hanging on only out of the need to keep the girls calm and steady. "You ruined everything."

"Rider shouldn't have come to my town." I was surprised I managed to keep my voice from shaking, at the rather blasé tone I used. Maybe I was getting more used to having my life threatened than I thought. Not a great claim to fame but at least it allowed me to fake confidence, something I needed a lot of to keep my knees from betraying me as we carried on through the garden path to the front of the house. "And neither should you, Joslyn."

She growled a bad word under her breath. "He was a fool," she snapped. "I tried so hard with him, but he never quite fell in line."

Wait, what? "He wasn't running the operation," I said then, now knowing exactly what was on that phone and in that cloud server that could bring her down. "You were."

She sniffed like it was insulting to consider otherwise. "The arrogant child," she said. "He had no idea what to do. I had all the connections." I glanced back as she tossed her head. I was getting really sick of that motion, the scent of her shampoo or perfume or whatever revolting me now. "I let him think he was in control because it made him pliable. But then he had to lose my merchandise." She sounded like she wished she could bring him back to life so she could kill him herself. "Do you have any idea how long it took me to build that network? And he destroyed it in a single afternoon chat with a police therapist in a crap-water town no one cares about." I almost laughed. I know, it sounds weird, but she was so annoyed, so confounded, it tweaked my hysteria to the precipice of giggles. "He lost me everything."

"That's why you had Lawson kill him," I said.

"He had to go. He only continued to be a liability." She grabbed my arm, turned me around to face her, nose almost touching mine. "When we reach my car, you're getting in the driver's seat. I'll get in the back. And I'll take you somewhere nice and quiet and show you how much I appreciate you interfering with my business." She snarled. "You'll never do it again."

"They'll know you murdered me," I said. Again with the dead calm cynicism. No idea where it came from, but I wasn't complaining.

She seemed taken aback by my attitude, but it wasn't going to stop her. "You think me a fool, like Rider and Lawson?" Joslyn snorted. "I'm already set up elsewhere." Of course, she was. She'd been planning this, hadn't she? "Greener pastures, lessons learned. Your little sheriff and those ridiculous staties won't catch me."

"The FBI will," I said. "My ex-husband is kind of an expert at finding people. Dog with a bone, in fact. He'll hunt you down and catch you, Joslyn. He'll never rest until he does." Did I know that for a fact? Actually, yes. Not necessarily to avenge me, though, but because that was Special Agent in Charge Trent Garret.

She did hesitate at that. While I had a terrible idea.

Like, worst idea ever. Okay, not the first time I'd had it, either, but she was right there and so was the gun and I know. I know. I'd been shot before doing something this stupid, but how could I resist when the opportunity was so tempting?

She must have seen my intent, sensed me tensing because she took a solid step back before I could make a grab for the gun, pointing it between my eyes. "Don't even think about it."

Well, too late, but okay. If you insist.

We finished our walk to the front of the house, Joslyn corralling us to take a peek around the edge of the stone wall. Where was Lloyd? Inside, helping the Andersons like a good butler. That didn't stop me from unfairly wishing he'd do his job and kick Joslyn's butt with some cool CIA operative moves. Instead, when she seemed satisfied with the view, she motioned for us to hurry, pushing me bodily forward, Calliope stumbling with the near dead weight of Thalia in her arms, her girlfriend out of it and muttering incoherently.

She needed a doctor now. Whatever was going on with her, she had to have medical attention, and soon. Except, as Joslyn pushed me against the SUV, handing me a set of keys, I noticed something odd.

Thalia's eyes opened slowly. Met mine. And winked.

Deceptive little… I almost grinned, though the surge of hope really wasn't all that deserved. Joslyn still had her gun and she still had us under its control. Whatever Thalia had in mind or was planning, it couldn't negate the fact there was still ample opportunity for the psycho to shoot one or all of us before getting away.

"Get in." Joslyn stepped back, clearly expecting me to climb into the driver's seat without a fight and I did consider it, but Thalia obviously had a plan, so instead of giving in, I gave my daughter and her girlfriend a chance to save me.

I had no other choice. I ducked.

Just as the gun went off.

I turned, pivoting away from Joslyn, almost falling but catching myself and making it upright again, dropping into a judo wrestling stance as if that would counteract a bullet.

Instead of Joslyn waving her weapon around, however, she was on the ground, groaning and clutching her shoulder while Calliope—my amazing, brave and beautiful daughter—covered her with the weapon Joslyn once used to threaten us while Thalia held up what looked like a pen.

"Abigail," she said, tossing me the metal implement, the back end now blackened. "Spies have the coolest gadgets. Including pen guns."

I was grinning wildly, like an idiot, utterly delighted, about to tell Thalia that Abigail would be so proud of her, when a hiccup in our successful wrap-up appeared in the form of Brin Anderson who lunged from the dark, surprising Calliope.

Seized the gun.

And pointed it at Joslyn who had recovered sufficiently to glare back at the young woman now threatening her.

"You murdered Evan," Brin said, voice shaking. "I knew it was you all along. And I'm going to kill you for it."

CHAPTER NINETEEN

Joslyn struggled to her feet, blood soaking into the black of her dress, making it even shinier, oddly, as dark as the fabric in the low light. "I ordered his death," she said, facing down the shaking Brin. "But Rider did the deed. He was going to talk to the DA." She shrugged, cried out a little in pain, panted. So, her show was all that, the agony of the bullet wound (and I could attest to that) far more than she was showing. "I had to stop him from exposing us."

Melanie joined us, weeping, but it was she who put her arms around Brin, who whispered hoarsely to her, words loud enough in the quiet night for all of us to hear. "Let Evan go, baby," she said. "Let Rider and Joslyn go. All of it. His death was never your fault. But if you shoot her, if you kill her, I'll lose you like I lost him and I just can't live with that." Brin turned her head to meet her mother's eyes, gun not shifting but her shaking reduced. "Let the courts see that justice is done and let's get our lives back."

Brin let out a soft moan and then nodded, handing the gun back to Calliope and hugging her mother.

"How quaint," Joslyn snarled.

"Shut up," my daughter snapped back. "Or I'll have Thalia shoot you again."

Was she coming back to us? Because the Vesterville heiress chose that moment to giggle. I hoped so, but we'd be finding out soon enough.

I'd never been happier to text someone in my entire life. While Brin stared at me when I fired off a *HELP* to Cherise. She looked up, met my eyes, hand going to her back pocket.

And showed me the last piece of the puzzle.

"You found Rider's phone," I said.

She nodded, bleak, handing it to me, though it took her a moment to release it even after she offered it up. We all ignored Joslyn's growling fury while Brin spoke.

"I knew it was his all along," she said. "You surprised me when you showed Lawson yours."

"You were already gone," I said.

"I held back," she admitted. "I wanted to hear what he had to say." She swallowed, looked to her mother. "I thought I'd made a mistake, but it *was* his." She shrugged. "I was going to break the security, download the proof myself. But I guess I don't need to." She sighed deeply, hands sliding into the pockets of her black skirt. "Now it belongs to the police." She shuddered a little, as though shedding some weight and faced Joslyn with a grin. "I'll be in court every day," she said, "and I'll laugh when they send you away for the rest of your life."

Joslyn didn't say a word, though I doubt we would have heard her over the sound of the sirens that cut the silence that followed, a Charger skidding to a halt with two cruisers—one state, one local—hot on the sheriff's heels.

The EMTs finished their patching up job, Joslyn loaded into the back of the ambulance, though I wasn't surprised when one of the deputies climbed in with her before driving off. Nor was I shocked when a large SUV pulled up the driveway at a rather excessive speed, barely parked and still running as Trent jumped out of the driver's side and ran toward me.

"I just landed," he said, desperate panic on his face. I'd never seen him look that way before, his FBI training giving him a morose stoicness that frustrated me with its lack of emotional generosity. I almost hugged him but held back as he went on. "Are Melanie and Brin okay?"

I honestly didn't know what to say. Stood there with my mouth hanging open, speechless as he caught sight of them and hurried past me to where they talked with Cherise. Bypassing (though, in hindsight, it would have been easy to miss Calliope and Thalia off to one side with Lloyd who stood in front of them like a guardian statue ready to take on all comers) his own daughter (did I mention I needed to be kind about the fact he didn't choose his flesh-and-blood first?) and making a beeline right for his girlfriend and her kid.

Choke. Splutter. Growl.

Momma Bear hadn't left the building yet, apparently.

As for Calliope, she didn't seem to care her father hadn't even seen her in his need to get to the Andersons. Instead, I could see her arguing with Thalia who seemed weak on her feet no matter her previous fake at being almost comatose. Since she'd spent the evening wavering between self-possessed belle of the ball and confused and nearly delirious, I was in my daughter's camp. Except as Calliope gestured toward the house, I marched in their direction, gesturing to Cherise to join me.

"You're not going back inside," I said. "Either of you."

Thalia blinked at me, wobbly on her feet but managing a smile so she wasn't the horrible bullying and careless woman she'd been during the party. She was Thalia, at least I hoped so. "I'm going to go lie down." At least, I think that was what she said because her words came out garbled and a little mixed up in order.

"Hospital," I snapped. "Now."

"Is everything okay?" Oh, so now Trent decided to join us. Typical. I ignored him, staring the girls down, letting Cherise handle him.

"Fine," she lied. "You didn't need to come. We had it handled." She snorted. "Seph and the girls did, actually."

I caught his startled expression out of the corner of my eye, but I wasn't sparing him even a second.

"Okay," he said then, sounding hesitant. "If you don't need me, I'll make sure Melanie and Brin get home safely." Why did I think that was all he cared about anyway? Forget it, I had two young women I loved more than anything in the world to wrangle and we were going to the hospital even if I had to throw Thalia over my shoulder and carry her on foot.

That would be a sight, but I'd do it and don't ever think otherwise.

Trent left after a long and awkward moment of silence, and I was glad. I'd deal with him and his callous disregard and lack of attention for his own freaking daughter after I'd handled whatever was happening with Thalia.

For her part, her rebellion had returned somewhat, though she continued to waver like she was out of steam and would collapse at any second. Perfect, because she'd have to sit and the front seat of my car was the ideal place for her to rest while I broke every speed law in Wallace to get to the ER.

"Mom." Calliope waved me off. "Give us a second, okay?"

Took a lot, like a lot. But I backed away, turned to Cherise, ready to choke someone. Only to face down her disappointment.

"What did I say about not getting shot at again?" She huffed a breath, shook her head before I could protest. This wasn't my fault. "Never mind," she said, tossing her hands.

"Looks like it runs in the family now. You happy?"

I didn't know what to say. No quippy comebacks surfaced. Instead, I shrugged.

That made my sheriff friend laugh, if in resignation instead of humor.

I purposely ignored Trent as he climbed back into his SUV, the Anderson's catering van following him out. They'd brought it around the front of the house while Joslyn was being treated, their exodus seemingly a trigger for Thalia.

"I don't need a hospital!" Cherise and I both turned back to find the Vesterville heiress shaking, pushing Calliope away, fury twisting her face into a mask I barely recognized. "Leave me alone! Don't you see?" She clenched her hands into fists, backing away from Lloyd who tried to support her, staggering, swaying, skirt askew, skirt untucked, hair unbound, in her stocking feet and looking more vulnerable and fragile than ever. And that head tilt was back, finally triggering a recollection in me that had me hoping I was wrong. "You need to go, Callie." She drove both hands into her hair, pulling on the long, pale strands, her voice rising. "You need to get away from me before the curse gets you too!"

Calliope ignored the order, reached for her, but Thalia shoved my daughter. In doing so, she stumbled, putting herself off balance. Hung like a teetering tower piled too high and out of order to remain upright. Whispered, "Callie," her expression taking on a shocked, wide-eyed look.

Before she collapsed slowly and almost elegantly to the cold ground, boneless and unconscious.

Almost. Calliope moved quickly enough to save her from the full impact of her fall, though the move carried my daughter to the ground under Thalia's slim weight. She looked up at me with tears pouring down her face. "Mom!"

I was at her side and Cherise already on the phone before the echo of her cry died.

CHAPTER TWENTY

The steady beeping of the heart monitor at least reassured me Thalia was with us, her rhythm normal enough, though it was clear there was something very wrong that therapy wasn't going to help.

She wasn't on drugs, and she wasn't having a psychotic break. That meant a physiological cause and though I prayed I didn't remember correctly, I was pretty sure I already knew her diagnosis.

The question was, could they treat it?

Her hand was so thin and cold in mine where I sat on her left, Calliope's chair pulled as close as she could get it on Thalia's right, clinging to her girlfriend's pale fingers between her own warm ones, the contrast between Calliope's tan and the Vesterville's striking. I could see the veins in Thalia's hand, pale blue under the transparency of her flesh even more pronounced, deep, dark circles under her closed eyes, breath coming in slow and steady inhales and exhales as she slept off her faint.

The white hospital gown and washed-out green sheets weren't improving her pallor any, but I did my best to just sit and not fret or fidget and be there for both of my girls while we waited to hear what the doctor had to say.

The fact they admitted Thalia the moment we arrived wasn't a surprise, since she'd been unconscious, though I'd expected them to set her up in the ER instead of finding her a room right away. Or that they'd then rushed her off to run a bunch of tests that she'd only just come back from. That didn't bode well, though she was a Vesterville, and part of the hospital was named for her father, so maybe that had something to do with it. I could hope it wasn't that they suspected what I now did and that was the reason she had her own room in critical care.

Reading too much into it, right?

My phone buzzed, a welcome distraction, Calliope resting her forehead on Thalia's upper arm as I checked it. Wished I hadn't because I wasn't ready to talk to him right now.

Is Calliope okay, Seph? Trent's first text had

me spitting mad all over again, though I was in an emotional state, I admit (and fair enough) so I may have been less willing to tear him a new one under different circumstances. *I'm sorry I left so quickly. Melanie and Brin have been through so much this past year with Evan's death. I promised them I'd find proof Rider Huntington killed him. Thank you for resolving that for them.*

Grumble. *Thalia's in the hospital.* That was a very mean text to send after what he'd shared, but too freaking bad. We'd both spent part of our marriage parenting her as much as we had Calliope. He should know what and who he abandoned for his new family.

Persephone Pringle. That was so beneath you. So?

He didn't respond. Maybe he didn't get it. Or maybe he didn't care. Whatever the reason, I was so grateful for the millionth time I was no longer married to Trent Freaking Garret.

Another text had me thinking he finally realized he was a jerk, but nope. This one was from Cherise.

I'm heading back to the hospital, she sent. She'd made sure we'd arrived safely before regretfully leaving for her office to liaise with the state police. I'd made her go, knew she had responsibilities but that she, at least cared (stop it right now, young lady). *Can I bring you two anything?*

Coffee, I sent. *Thank you, Cherise. I think it's going to be a long night.*

Five minutes, she sent. *Love to Callie.*

I didn't get to share the sentiment, Thalia groaning softly cutting off the outside world completely before she squeezed my hand as she opened her eyes. Our smiling, if teary, faces were the first things she saw, and I wouldn't have had it any other way.

"What… what happened?" She smiled back at me, then Calliope who couldn't stop herself from sobbing once, shaking as she leaned in and kissed her girlfriend very gently on the forehead. "Did I shoot someone?"

I coughed an unexpected laugh. "You and Abigail saved my life," I said. "How did you know about the pen?"

She turned her head to look at me, that wonderous smile lingering. "After what happened last year, I did a lot of research into Abigail," she said. "She was an amazing woman, Seph. I was curious, so I studied all her spy gadgets." She eye-rolled. "I even learned how to clean and load the pen gun. That's how I knew it would work." She tried to shrug but her left shoulder didn't rise, head tilting to the side in a slow fall toward Calliope though she continued to stare me in the eyes. "What's wrong with me?"

I shook my head, lower lip trembling, the burning in the back of my throat tightening so much I couldn't speak very loudly. "I don't know, honey," I said.

"But I do." I spun at the new voice interrupting us, a middle-aged woman in a white lab coat nodding to us from the doorway, her stethoscope draped around her neck, Dr. Sandra Jessup stitched in blue over her left chest pocket. "I'm Dr. Jessup, Thalia." She crossed the room to stand at the foot of the bed, one hand clutching a smart tablet, her soothing alto only making me more nervous. "I'm your primary oncologist while you're with us. Do you know what that means?

"Dr. Jessup," Calliope said, voice shaking, and bypassing the question altogether while I knew the answer very well. After all, my father had an oncologist, though his prognosis meant a rapid decline despite treatment. "You said you know what's wrong?" She and Thalia exchanged a look, their fingers interlocking, though when they both turned back to meet the doctor's eyes, it was as one. Whatever rift had come about thanks to Thalia's condition, it no longer existed, and I knew then, no matter what came next, they had each other to the end.

As long as that end didn't come sooner

rather than later.

Please.

Jumping to conclusions again, Seph.

"I want to show you something." She turned as she touched the screen in her hand, linking up to the large TV monitor hung on the wall across from Thalia. It blinked to life, black background detailing what looked like a brain scan. I spotted the anomaly immediately, caught myself from crying by biting the inside of my cheek as the doctor firmly but kindly explained what I suspected and now knew was true.

"Thalia, you have a brain tumor." Dr. Jessup pointed out the pale mass on the bottom left-hand side of Thalia's scan. "As you can see, it's located near the amygdala, the control center for emotion." She pointed out the area by drawing a circle around it on her tablet, instantly transmitting to the larger screen. "That's why you found it difficult to control how you were feeling, the shift in personality, and, as Ms. Pringle pointed out, why you have been tilting your head. The tumor is influencing your actions."

No one said a word for a long moment. To my surprise, it was Calliope who spoke first, voice calm despite the news. How she managed it I had no idea, because there was no way I could have gotten a word out in that moment.

"How do you treat it?" Bless her for going right to optimistic when it was clear from the crumpling trying to take over Thalia's face she wasn't even close to hope.

"I may have some good news on that front," Dr. Jessup said. "The rapidity of your transformation suggests the tumor might be a rapidly growing cyst, which could be benign or malignant, but I'm hopeful it's the former. If so, we drain the cyst and remove the sac that contains it. That should end the issue completely." She set the tablet on the end of the bed, her expression settling into compassion but with firm conviction. "There is a chance it's malignant," she said. "In which case, we would also need to implement radiation and chemotherapy. However, if I'm wrong and this is a tumor, it will require extensive surgery to remove the mass. And could damage the tissue permanently, leading to changes in personality and mobility."

Both girls stared at her this time, still clinging to each other while I finally took over.

"When will you know if it's a cyst, Dr. Jessup?"

She almost seemed relieved to speak to me. "We'll do another MRI shortly, but I'm fairly confident that's what we're looking at. Once that's done, we'll book the OR and test the cyst for fluid. At that point, we'll proceed depending on what we find." She lifted her tablet again, holding it in both hands. "You've been through a lot today, from what I understand." Did she know about the murder? Didn't matter. "I'll let you get some rest, Thalia. But we need to act on this quickly. I'll have some paperwork for you to sign. If you have any further questions, please don't hesitate to ask for me." She nodded to me, to the girls, and left.

Just like that.

"At least we know now," Calliope said, wiping her tears on her pirate shirt.

"We do." Thalia's previous response had faded, a resigned expression, almost peaceful, settling over her face. "The Vesterville curse strikes again."

Not even I knew how to counter that.

I sighed my way into the entry, Belladonna hurrying toward me, chirping the entire way. The moment she reached me I lifted her into my arms, carrying her to the kitchen. Poured myself a very tall gin with just a little cranberry because it had been that kind of day.

It took two long drinks before I turned and went back to the other end of the house, to my office. Sat at my computer, thinking for a very long time about what to do next. Thought about Cherise arriving a moment after the doctor left, her tears and hugs for the girls, how we'd all sat and talked for a little while before Thalia fell asleep. And though I'd insisted Calliope come home with me, she'd fought back.

"I'm going to be here when she wakes up, Mom," my daughter said. "Just go. I'll see you tomorrow."

How did I leave my brave girl all alone like that? I still debated with a heavy heart about going back while Belladonna purred and kneaded in my lap, refusing to settle.

"You know something's up, don't you?" I stroked her soft fur, sipping my gin, feeling the warmth of it finally relax me. Had a good cry, about a nice ten-minute sob fest with tons of tissues and nose blowing and purging of grief and guilt while my cat comforted me with her heavy, healing purr.

By the time I was done with the pity party, I was tipsy. Not that it stopped me from booting up my computer and opening my email. Addressing a message to the anonymous account I'd come into possession of almost a year ago.

Drew a deep breath before typing the bad news.

Thalia has a brain tumor. She's in the hospital. The doctor is investigating, and she seems optimistic that it's treatable, but your niece needs you.

I sat back from that. Did she, though? She had Calliope and me, Cherise, Lloyd. He hadn't been in her life much at all, even when she was little. But I knew if I didn't message him, he'd never forgive me. And he wasn't the kind of person you wanted mad at you, especially where his niece was concerned.

Thalia's super-secret spy uncle had killed before and, I had zero doubt, had since we'd seen each other last. No way was I putting myself on his hit list. And he really did deserve to know.

I hit send, sat back, exhaled. Waited. Knew it wouldn't be long.

It wasn't.

I'm on my way, Gaines Vesterville sent.

I turned off my computer and hugged my cat, hoping I hadn't just made a terrible decision.

There's more Persephone Pringle coming, but, for now, why not check out my list of cozies? I have a large selection of contemporary and paranormal murder mysteries available at **https://pattilarsen.com/home** and at all fine retailers!

ABOUT THE AUTHOR

Everything you need to know about me is in this one statement: I've wanted to be a writer since I was a little girl, and now I'm doing it. How cool is that, being able to follow your dream and make it reality? I've tried everything from university to college, graduating the second with a journalism diploma (I sucked at telling real stories), am an enthusiastic member of an all-girl improv troupe (if you've never tried it, I highly recommend making things up as you go along as often as possible) and I get to teach and perform with an amazing group of women I adore. I've even been in a Celtic girl band (some of our stuff is on YouTube!) and was an independent filmmaker. You can check out the whole Lovely Witches Club series for free at:

https://lovelywitchesclub.com.

My life has been one creative thing after another—all leading me here, to writing books for a living.

Now with multiple series in happy publication, I live on beautiful and magical Prince Edward Island (I know you've heard of Anne of Green Gables) with my multitude of pets.

I love-love-love hearing from you! You can reach me (and I promise I'll message back) at https://patti@pattilarsen.com/home. And if you're eager for your next dose of Patti Larsen books (usually about one release a month) come join my mailing list! All the best up and coming, giveaways, contests and, of course, my observations on the world (aren't you just dying to know what I think about everything?) all in one place:

https://bit.ly/PattiLarsenEmail.

Last—but not least!—I hope you enjoyed what you read! Your happiness is my happiness. And I'd love to hear just what you thought. A review where you found this book would mean the world to me—reviews feed writers more than you will ever know. So, loved it (or not so much), your honest review would make my day. Thank you!